Christmas in Gracechurch Street

Christmas in Gracechurch Street

A Darcy and Elizabeth Variation

LEENIE BROWN

LEENIE B BOOKS
HALIFAX

Cover design by Leenie B Books. Images sourced from Deposit Photos and Period Images.

Christmas in Gracechurch Street © 2020 Leenie Brown. All Rights Reserved, except where otherwise noted.

ISBN (print) 978-1-989410-70-7, (large print) 978-1-989410-71-4; (ebook) 978-1-989410-69-1

Contents

Prologue

The morning of November 20, 1811

Mr. Bennet tucked Mr. Gardiner's letter into his pocket and rose from the breakfast table in anticipation of his wife's response to the news he had just shared with her.

"What do you mean my brother has requested for Elizabeth and Mary to visit him?" Mrs. Bennet demanded just as her husband had expected she would. After all these years, she had yet to surprise him too much with her reactions to various bits of news.

"Come with me, my dear. We shall discuss this in private." He took his wife by the elbow, excused them from the breakfast room, and steered her across the hall to the sitting room where he closed and locked the door. Then, he once again took her by the elbow and moved them both as far from the door as possible, for he knew that conversations were often listened to through keyholes.

"Your brother has requested for them to visit him because I asked him to take them."

It was a calculated move. Just two days ago, he had heard his wife discussing the generous olive branch that his cousin, Mr. Collins, presented, and there was no way he was going to give *that* man an opportunity to propose to Elizabeth.

Mrs. Bennet gasped. "Why would you do that? We have a guest who holds a valuable living and is in need of a wife."

The match was ridiculous – not in means of wealth or inheritance but in the fact that Mr. Collins was a fool, and Elizabeth was the opposite. As much as Mr. Bennet wished to share his amusement at the gentleman's foibles and follies with his favourite daughter, he could not be a party to her being put upon to marry the man. She would refuse, of course, and then, well, that olive branch would become the very fuel used to fan the flames of former displeasure.

"You may present him with Kitty or Lydia."

"Kitty or Lydia?" Mrs. Bennet fairly cried. "I

think not! They are far too lively and pretty to set-tle for a parson."

"Then, you shall have to content yourself with none of your daughters marrying my cousin."

"But what of me? Who shall see to my care when you are gone?"

That was always her concern, and no matter how many times he explained to her that she would not be left destitute when he died, she could not grasp anything beyond the fact that Longbourn would no longer be her home.

"Why, Mr. Bingley, of course. That is if you can convince him to take Jane. After all, his seeming interest in our eldest daughter, combined with your skill at drawing a gentleman along, is precisely why I am allowing her to remain at home."

Mrs. Bennet smiled slightly at the comment. "I suppose you are correct about that. Jane would never see me go without."

And neither would he, but this was not the time for that discussion. "Indeed, she would not. Jane is far too generous and kind."

"And beautiful," Mrs. Bennet said on a sigh. "However, who will have Lizzy if Mr. Collins does not?"

"None of your daughters lack for beauty, my dear. There will be a gentleman who will have Elizabeth. She is young. There is time."

"She is so difficult."

"Aye, she is that at times, but no more so than Lydia." His wife did not look convinced, but there was yet one more weapon in his arsenal. "Did you know that Lady Catherine de Bourgh is the sister of the Earl of Matlock?"

His wife's brow furrowed.

"I did some inquiring about her from Mr. Collins while we played backgammon the other night, and then, I did a little questioning of Mr. Bingley while I was out yesterday. His sister ordered some lovely lace, by the by. I assume it is for a dress – perhaps the one that she intends to wear to her brother's ball."

"Did she? What did it look like?"

Mr. Bennet shook his head. "I did not see it. I only heard about it, and I would have been far happier to have not heard about it at all." However, it had been necessary to hear of Miss Bingley's lace during his and Mr. Bingley's conversation so that he could discover what he wished.

"Oh." There was disappointment in Mrs. Bennet's tone.

"I also discovered that we have a neighbour who claims the Earl of Matlock as his uncle."

Her eyebrows flew up. "We do?"

Mr. Bennet nodded and leaned toward his wife as he whispered, "Mr. Darcy."

"Mr. Darcy?" Her hand rested on her heart.

Again, Mr. Bennet nodded.

"Truly? I knew he was wealthy, but an earl for an uncle? That is something." She paused as if lost in thought. "Do you suppose he could like Jane?"

Mr. Bennet chuckled. "Have you so soon forgotten how he spoke about Lizzy? Are you certain Jane would do well with such a disagreeable gentleman?"

Disappointment settled visibly on his wife's features. "No, I suppose she would not."

"And do you suppose, my dear, that a gentleman such as Mr. Darcy would approve of his friend marrying the sister of his aunt's parson?"

Mrs. Bennet's mouth dropped open. "I had not thought of that."

Mr. Bennet waited patiently while the disaster that such a thought presented settled into his wife's mind. He knew the moment it did, for she gasped and immediately started for the door while declaring, "There is much to be done! You will have to write to my brother and tell him that Mary will require a bit of lace for her dresses."

And so, it was settled and determined that Elizabeth, accompanied by her sister Mary, were to be made ready to go to town by the following morning just as their father had planned.

Chapter 1

The Afternoon of November 29, 1811

Rain beat a steady pattern on the sidewalk and all who were dashing to and fro as Fitzwilliam Darcy ducked into the store and out of the weather. He removed his hat and did his best to leave any traces of the day's dampness at the door before joining his sister who was waiting for him just two steps away.

Although he was happy to see his sister once again taking an interest in the things she had always loved to do, accompanying her on a shopping excursion was not why he had returned to town sooner than expected.

"Will we have Christmas at Darcy House or Netherfield?" Georgiana placed her gloved hand on his arm when he offered it to her.

"Do you not wish to go to Pemberley?" He had hoped she would.

"Oh, look at that pair of gloves, Fitzwilliam." She tugged him toward a display case where a clerk was just returning a pair of kid gloves to the display. "Are they not the most divine gloves you have ever seen?"

"No."

"Fitzwilliam," her tone was slightly scolding, "do try to be interested in things."

"I find many things interesting, Georgiana. It is just that the divineness of a pair of gloves is not amongst those things."

She held his gaze and fluttered her lashes.

He might not know if a particular pair of gloves was divine or not, but he did recognize that expression. "Will this bit of perfection make you happy?"

Her smile was answer enough.

He glanced at the clerk and gave a nod.

The gloves were speedily returned to the top of the case.

"Will they make you happy enough to go home?"

Her brow furrowed and her lips pursed. Apparently, the gloves were not that perfect.

"We have only just arrived," she retorted as she tried one of the gloves on and sighed with pleasure.

"We have patronized three establishments already. Therefore, if we only see four display cases instead of all of them in this store, I think we can leave with a sense of accomplishment. John cannot hold many more packages."

She removed the glove and laid it on the glass top of the counter. "We could have whatever we find here delivered, and you could allow John to go home now."

"And I suppose that we will just wait for the carriage to return?" He raised an eyebrow at her.

She shrugged. "It was just a suggestion."

"Shall I wrap them?" the clerk asked.

"Please," Darcy answered before turning back to his sister. "As delighted as I am with the fact that your desire to spend my money has returned, could we please be done soon?" He was spoiling her again. He knew he was.

As the purchase of the gloves was completed and yet another parcel was entrusted to John, Georgiana smiled her sweet smile at Darcy – the one he thought had been lost thanks to a cad who had broken her heart – patted his arm, and assured him that she would be ready to go just as soon as she procured a bottle of fragrance.

"You never told me if you wish to go to Pemberley for Christmas," he said as he directed them further into the store toward the display of bottles and boxes of fragrance.

"I am surprised you are even asking. I thought you made arrangements to not return to Pemberley until the spring."

"I did, but if you would like to go to Pemberley for Christmas, I would be happy to take you." Very happy, truth be told. The further he was away from Hertfordshire, the better. He had hoped that returning to town after Bingley's ball would be the escape he needed. However, when Miss Elizabeth Bennet did not attend that ball and Darcy discovered it was because she was in town, any escape that was in his plan had evaporated into thin air.

"I thought we could invite Bingley and his sisters to join us."

Georgiana turned away from the clerk who was wafting fragrance in her direction.

Darcy sniffed. The fragrance smelled familiar. His eyes grew wide as he realized of whom it reminded him.

Whatever protest Georgiana was going to make about the Bingleys spending Christmas with them at Pemberley died on her lips. "Do you not like this fragrance?"

"No, no. It is beautiful." With just a hint less lavender than what he had smelled on Miss Elizabeth on the mornings when she had stayed at Netherfield.

"Shall I buy some?"

He swallowed. "If you would like," he managed to answer calmly while hoping with all that was in him that it was not what she would like.

"I have admired it for some time, and Mrs. Annesley thought it would be fine for someone my age when we were here last week." The uncertainty in her eyes begged him to make the decision for her.

"Then, if you admire it and Mrs. Annesley approves, you should get a bottle." He would just have to not think of Miss Elizabeth Bennet whenever his sister wore it.

"Are you certain? You looked pained."

"We have been shopping for some time now, Georgiana. I am pained." Of course, being reminded of Miss Elizabeth did not help lessen his discomfort. However, he was not about to admit that to his sister. He was admitting it to himself, but he was doing so most unwillingly.

"Fitzwilliam," she scolded.

"It is a lovely fragrance. Please wrap up a bottle for us," he said to the clerk.

His sister was studying him when he turned back to her.

"Does it remind you of Mother?" she asked in a whisper.

He shook his head. "No, someone else."

Her eyebrows rose, and she blinked.

"Now," he said before she could ask him about his confession, "I believe that you promised we could go home just as soon as you got a bottle of fragrance." He thanked the clerk and handed the wrapped parcel to John, who stuffed it in his pocket. Then, Darcy offered his arm to his sister once again.

"About Pemberley," he began as they made their way through the store.

"I do not want to go to Pemberley."

"You do not?" He had been so sure she would be willing to return to their Derbyshire estate. She had always loved Christmas there.

"No. I would like to see Netherfield."

"I do not think that is a good idea." And not just because it was only three miles from Longbourn and Miss Elizabeth, once she returned home, but also because a certain ne'er-do-well was part of the militia regiment which was quartered in Meryton.

Her brow furrowed, and he actually longed to stay inside the store so that he would have a reason to not answer the question he knew she was going to ask. He did not want to tell her than he had seen Mr. Wickham. She was smiling again. She did not need to hear about the man who had broken her heart.

"I will explain in the carriage," he offered before she could ask.

As much as he did not wish to speak of Mr. Wickham, he knew he must. No matter how he wished it was not true, his sister was no longer a child. She was one season away from being a debutante, and who knew how long it would be after she made her debut before she would be someone's wife. The thought made his heart pinch. He was not ready to have her gone from his care, and, if he were to be honest with himself, which he knew he must be, he was fearful of her marrying the wrong gentleman and not being happy. After all, it had been *his* decision to hire her former companion – the one who had made it possible for Wickham to play with and break Georgiana's heart. And because of that error in judgment, he questioned his ability to guide her in selecting the correct husband.

He assisted her into the carriage and then, as he settled himself into his seat and the door was closed, he made his unvarnished explanation. "I saw Mr. Wickham when I was in Hertfordshire. He has joined the militia."

Georgiana sank back against the squabs. "Oh," was all she said.

He watched her face. She was clearly surprised but she did not look overly distressed.

The carriage lurched into motion as it progressed slowly down the street.

"Did he look well?" she finally asked.

"Unfortunately, yes."

Her lips tipped up just a touch into a small smile. "I do not wish him ill, Fitzwilliam."

"I do," Darcy answered honestly.

"I know, and I love you for it."

"He treated you abominably." Playing at courting her and loving her to gain access to her money!

"I most heartily agree, but I was naïve enough to allow it."

"You were fifteen! You were allowed to be naïve – in fact, I would say it is expected that one so young should be innocent enough to be thought naïve." Just the thought of that man made him want to punch something. He was positive that his reaction to seeing Wickham in Meryton had not left a good impression on Miss Elizabeth. However, leaving without speaking had seemed a better thing to do than jumping from his horse and pummeling the man into the ground as he had wished to do.

The carriage fell into silence for a full five minutes.

"He would not be at Netherfield, would he?"

"No. Neither he nor you will be at Netherfield."

"But your descriptions of Netherfield were so lovely. I would dearly love to see it," Georgiana pleaded.

Darcy shook his head. It was not a good idea. "You would likely have to hear about him, and if you went into the village, you might have to see and speak to him. It is too soon."

"But if you were with me…" her voice trailed off when he skewered her with a pointed look.

"I am sorry, Georgiana. I simply cannot put you in harm's way."

She nodded sullenly, and once again, silence reigned.

Darcy tipped his head back and closed his eyes. Not only could he not put his sister in harm's way, he also could not put himself there. Miss Elizabeth, contrary to what he had first said about her, was tempting – and lively and intelligent and caring. She was rather quite perfect if one did not consider her family, although her youngest sisters had been very nearly well-behaved at Bingley's ball.

"Who is she?"

Darcy's head snapped forward. "Who is who?"

"The lady that my new fragrance reminds you of."

"No one. Just an acquaintance." He tipped his head back again.

"From town?"

"No."

"From Hertfordshire?"

"It is really nothing worthy of such an interrogation, Georgie." He peeked at her. She was smiling.

"Then, I will not ask you about her again."

Darcy brought his head forward. "You will not?" That was a little unlike her. Not that he was unhappy that she would not ask again.

She shook her head and then turned the conversation as if to prove the truth of her statement. "Will we have Lord and Lady Matlock to dinner during the Christmas season?"

"I suppose we must."

Georgiana laughed. "You say that as if you do not like them."

"I do not like our aunt's constant comments about my needing a wife." Thankfully, Lady Matlock did not have a daughter she was trying to convince him to marry. That special position was held by his other aunt, Lady Catherine de Bourgh.

"You will need one eventually." Her comment sounded a great deal like something Lady Matlock would say.

"I know my duty," he replied, just as he would to his aunt, "but I would like to determine when and who without interference from either of our aunts." He leaned his head back only to bring it forward once more. "Nor do I wish for Miss Bingley's help."

Once again, Georgiana laughed. "Caroline is not so very bad, and she is accomplished."

He shook his head. Georgiana had not seen the truly cunning and cutting side of Miss Bingley. "She would drive me to Bedlam. I swear she does not have an original thought in her head. All she ever does is agree with me." And point out what other ladies lacked.

"Fitzwilliam, that is what we are supposed to do."

"No, it is not – no matter what your aunt or Miss Annesley might say to the contrary – not all men want such agreeable wives. Some of us wish for ladies who can argue and reason." He could think of one beguiling lady who fit that description perfectly.

"Such ladies are often impertinent," Georgiana said.

"Delightfully so," he replied without thought.

"Indeed? Does that mean I may be argumentative and impertinent?"

"No, it does not." He scrubbed his face. "However, you seem to be doing an excellent job of being both at present."

"You cannot say they are traits to be admired and traits to be avoided at the same time. Which is it, Fitzwilliam?"

"I do not know," he answered truthfully. He wished he did. He wished he could say that no lady ever should be argumentative and impertinent, but he could not say that because he found those attributes to be downright enticing when presented to him in the form of Miss Elizabeth Bennet. "For now, could you refrain from being argumentative and impertinent. I did go shopping with you, after all." He scrubbed his face again.

The carriage slowed and drew to a stop in front of Darcy House.

"Mr. Bingley is here."

Darcy leaned forward to look out the window with his sister and groaned. There, on his front step, was Bingley, with his arms crossed and a scowl on his face.

"He does not look pleased," Georgiana said as the steps were put into place. "Perhaps we should have stopped at one more store."

"Indeed," Darcy said as he climbed out of the

carriage. He suspected that looking at frills and fripperies would be more easily endured than Bingley's displeasure.

"Imagine my surprise to find my sisters were in town this morning," Bingley said by way of a greeting.

"We returned early for Christmas and to prepare for the season."

"I am telling you what I told them," Bingley continued as if Darcy had not said a word. "I am returning to Netherfield whether you go with me or not." He nodded to Georgiana. "How are you today, Miss Darcy?"

"I am quite well, and I would ask the same of you except that I can see you are not completely well. Will you come in for a while?"

He glanced at Darcy and cocked an eyebrow over accusing eyes.

"We would be happy to have your company," Darcy assured him. Happy was perhaps a bit of a stretch. Normally, Darcy liked nothing better than an evening at home with Georgiana and a close friend such as Bingley, however, at present, he would much happier to not have to endure Bingley's glares and scolds.

"So long as it is in town," Bingley muttered with a pointed look that caused Darcy's ears to burn. "You know Miss Bennet is a gentleman's daughter do you not?" He added as he followed the Darcy siblings into Darcy House.

"Yes, I am aware of that fact, and should she favor you, it would not be an intolerable match."

Bingley grinned at the comment. "Then, wish me happy."

"I beg your pardon?" What was the man talking about?

"She favours me."

"I saw no sign of it," Darcy countered.

"I have had the good news from her sister."

Darcy shook his head. "I still do not understand what you are saying. Which sister has told you this and how did you get such intelligence from her? You are not keeping up a correspondence with one of the Bennet ladies are you?"

"Do you take me for a fool?" Bingley snapped but then held up his hand. "Do not answer that. I will. I am not a fool. I might fall in love easily and assume that I am loved in return without proof on occasion, but this is not one of those occasions. Miss Bennet is the lady for me, and, after calling in

Gracechurch Street and hearing from Miss Elizabeth that Miss Bennet was distraught at my departure, I have nothing to fear. I am not imagining what I wish this time, my friend."

"You called on Miss Elizabeth?" Darcy's palms felt damp. Thinking about Miss Elizabeth was one thing. Knowing she was in town was another step in the direction of disconcerting. But hearing about her, placed him directly in the middle of discomfiture.

Bingley nodded. "And Miss Mary. The Gardiners are quite genteel. I believe you would like them, Darcy." He clapped his friend on the back. "I accepted an invitation to dine at their house tomorrow on your behalf. I declined on the behalf of my sisters since I am too displeased with them to allow them to join me anywhere."

"But you accepted on my behalf?" And things had moved from uncomfortable to vexatious.

Bingley nodded and looked utterly pleased that Darcy was not happy. "Mrs. Gardiner seemed anxious to meet you. She hales from Lambton."

"She does?" Darcy felt as if the earth under his feet had shifted.

"I mentioned you might be loathed to leave your sister."

Darcy's eyes narrowed.

"Am I invited, too?" Georgiana asked eagerly.

"You do not like meeting new people," Darcy reminded her. True, she was not as reticent to the prospect as he was. She had been a shy child, but she was no longer a child.

"If Mr. Bingley recommends them, I think I shall like meeting them quite well." Her lashes fluttered over amused eyes. "And, it sounds, Brother, as if you can tell me something about two of the people I will meet."

"Indeed, he can. He is quite well-acquainted with Miss Elizabeth, but he knows less about Miss Mary," Bingley said. "If you wish, I can describe Mrs. Gardiner to you, and I have met two of her children. The other two were in the nursery, and her husband was at his warehouse. However, she assures me that he will be overjoyed to have a fine gathering of people around his table tomorrow."

"He sounds friendly," Georgiana said.

"If he is anything like his wife, he will be excessively welcoming."

"You said he has a warehouse?" Georgiana

placed her hand on Bingley's arm and moved toward the drawing room.

"More than one. I gather he is rather wealthy. You can see one of his warehouses from his home."

"How interesting!" Georgiana sounded perfectly delighted by the prospect of meeting the Gardiners.

Darcy was less delighted. "Tomorrow? Must it be tomorrow?" he called after Bingley.

"Yes, and do not try to avoid going. I am too displeased with you to allow you to beg off."

Darcy blew out a breath. Apparently, tomorrow, he was going to be forced into company once again with Miss Elizabeth. He would never again trust himself to devise a plan of escape, for, apparently, it was not a skill he possessed.

Chapter 2

The long shadows of evening were chasing away the last remains of the afternoon sun while Elizabeth Bennet sat on the edge of the bed that she was sharing with her sister Mary at her aunt and uncle's house in Gracechurch Street. She was not, however, admiring her sister's hair as Mary added some pretty pins to it, nor was she considering what dress she would wear to dinner. She was, in fact, wishing that she could climb into bed and have a tray brought to her room. She would not even mind if her dinner were just tea and toast if it meant that she would not have to see Mr. Darcy.

"I wish Mr. Darcy was not coming," she admitted aloud.

Mary looked in her direction. "You are not still holding his words against him, are you?"

"How can I not?" That was not why she wished

he was not coming, but it seemed a good enough excuse for not wishing to see the gentleman.

Mary cocked an eyebrow. "The better question is how can you still?"

"It was not you whom he called not handsome enough."

The way Mr. Darcy's eyes had been so cold when he looked in her direction and said those horrible words was not something she could easily forget. She had hoped he would ask her to dance. She had even suggested to Jane that perhaps her partner Mr. Bingley could make the introduction and facilitate the pleasure of a dance. However, instead of a half-hour of conversation and dancing, she had been left to sit and watch others while attempting to not care about Mr. Darcy's cutting remarks concerning her.

"And what has Jane said about him? Neither she nor I believe Mr. Darcy can truly be so bad if he is Mr. Bingley's friend." Mary joined Elizabeth on the bed. "Did I do it right?" She tipped and turned her head for her sister's approval.

Elizabeth smiled. "Yes, your hair looks lovely."

Mary was not usually the sort of lady to care about her looks. Neat and tidy were her normal criteria for being presentable. However, having been sent to town seemed to have worked some sort of magic on Elizabeth's younger sister. Mary had, uncharacteristically, fretted over which dresses to bring when she was preparing to travel, and, since arriving at the Gardiners, she had taken much greater care to present herself in a more becoming fashion than was her normal wont.

"I know that there will not be any new gentlemen callers tonight, as I have met both Mr. Darcy and Mr. Bingley, but," Mary lowered her voice as if fearful of saying what she was about to say, "I have not met Miss Darcy. I would imagine she is a very fashionable young lady."

"I suppose she is," Elizabeth agreed.

"I would like for her to like me."

"Why?" Normally, Mary did not care if anyone liked her, or, at least, that is how it had always appeared to Elizabeth. In fact, Elizabeth had been somewhat jealous of Mary's ability not to place a great deal of importance on the opinions of others.

"I would very much like to call her my friend when she comes with her brother to visit Mr. Bingley. Mr. Darcy cannot leave his sister home every time he visits, can he?"

Elizabeth's brow furrowed. She was still not completely certain she understood what Mary was saying. "I do not know what their relationship is like, but it seems logical that Mr. Darcy might bring Miss Darcy with him at some point. However, I still do not see why you need to impress her."

Mary sighed. "That is because you have friends. I do not. Not one. Even in our family, you have Jane and Lydia has Kitty while I have nobody."

Mary's words caused Elizabeth to exhale much as a good thump of a pillow to her abdomen might. "Oh, Mary!" She put an arm around her sister. "Have you always felt lonely?"

Mary shook her head. "Not always, but often."

"What a horrid sister I have been!"

"No, do not say that," Mary protested. "I know that I should be content with my lot in life, but I find it challenging at times. Therefore, since it seems the good Lord has provided a holiday in London, I thought He might also provide me with either a friend or a gentleman caller while I am here." She ducked her head and smiled. "I would like a friend, this is true, but I would ever so much more greatly prefer a gentleman caller. Perhaps even one who might consider me as a possible wife."

"You wish to marry?" Elizabeth could not keep the surprise from her tone. Mary had never before mentioned anything about wanting to marry. She had always protested that her younger sisters and mother thought entirely too much about husbands and homes.

"I always have," Mary admitted.

"But you scold Lydia…"

"Because Lydia is annoying. All she ever thinks about is how handsome a gentleman is – and do not even mention a scarlet coat to me."

A small burst of laughter escaped Elizabeth. "I thought you were serious about only considering marriage once you were twenty-five and that you would only consider it then because it seemed the sensible thing to do. Was that all a ruse?"

A smile suffused Mary's face. "It is a good one, is it not? I spent many hours practising and perfecting it."

Elizabeth could not believe what she was hearing. Did she know her younger sister at all? "What else have you been hiding?"

"A great deal, I fear. Presenting myself as I always

have seemed a marvelous plan when I first set upon it. However, as I am approaching nineteen and have yet to have a gentleman call on me, I believe my plan was short-sighted. While my scheme worked masterfully to keep Mama from pushing me towards any gentlemen, it also seems to have made me unapproachable, for I spend almost every assembly sitting and watching others dance."

Was Mary, the sister who protested loudly about having to attend assemblies and balls, saying that she wished to dance? "But you do not like to dance!"

"That is true. I do not, but I would like to hold a gentleman's hand and stand close to him." There was a wistfulness to her tone. "I have known for some time now that my plan might have a fatal flaw, but I did not know how to change who I was at home. However, being here gives me the perfect opportunity to effect a transformation. I have never been sent to town before, so it could not have happened before now. Do you see?"

Elizabeth shook her head in disbelief. "I would ask if you are always so scheming, but from what you have told me, it seems you are."

"You do not hate me, do you?"

"Why should I hate you?"

"For being scheming."

"If I were to hate everyone who was scheming, I would have very few relations left to love." Elizabeth tilted her head and studied her sister. "Have you considered that perhaps if you had not changed yourself to torment our mother and Lydia, you might already have friends?"

Mary's face pinched in a grimace. "I did say I was beginning to think my plan was short-sighted." She sighed. "I am not so clever as you, Lizzy."

Elizabeth wrapped her arms around Mary and hugged her tightly. "I am not so clever. It is all a trick."

Mary giggled, which was a rather un-Mary-like thing to do. "It is not. You are clever."

"Clever does not make one pretty," she said as she released Mary. "And since it seems we are sharing secrets, then I must admit that there are times when I would rather be pretty than clever."

"Say something," Elizabeth added when Mary responded by simply staring at her.

"You are pretty."

Elizabeth closed her eyes. It would be easier to admit this part without having to see Mary's look of shock. Her cheeks grew warm even before she spoke. This was perhaps her most closely guarded secret. Not even Jane knew this. She blew out a breath. "I am not pretty enough."

With her eyes still closed, she waited for Mary to draw the appropriate conclusion.

"Not pretty enough for what?"

She groaned softly. She was going to have to say it. She did not want to say it. "For Mr. Darcy." There. It had been said. Embarrassment engulfed Elizabeth. Her cheeks were on fire and it felt as if tears just might find their way out of her eyes and down her cheeks at any moment.

"You like him?"

Elizabeth nodded. As much as she did not want to like Mr. Darcy, she did. No matter how many times she had proclaimed him horrible to try to convince herself that he was, it seemed she was not easily convinced about anything by anyone – not even when it was herself trying to do the convincing.

"Oh, well, is this not Providential?" Mary cried.

"How so?" Elizabeth asked, opening her eyes to see a delighted Mary crossing the room to their shared wardrobe.

"I am not so good at fashion, but I will do my best to help you present yourself as more than tolerable tonight," she said with a smile. "Is it not fabulous that we were sent to town and that Mr. Darcy just happens to be here?"

Fabulous was not a word Elizabeth would use.

"That is why it is Providential," Mary explained. "I learned a thing or two while reading all those dreadfully dull sermons to torment Lydia." She stood with the wardrobe door open behind her. "You and Mr. Darcy are destined to be together. It is the will of the good Lord." She turned toward the wardrobe.

"Mary."

"Yes." She peeked over her shoulder at Elizabeth.

"You are sounding a lot like Mama but with words that the parson would use thrown in."

"I suppose I am, but Mama is not always wrong." She smiled. "I know I have often disagreed with her." Her brow furrowed and her lips pursed. "No, that is not accurate. I have nearly always disagreed with her. It was another part of my ill-thought-out plan."

Elizabeth was not certain if she preferred this

new Mary to the old Mary. "Mr. Darcy does not like me."

"I do not believe it," Mary said from where she had her head inside the wardrobe looking at dresses. "He was not rude to you at Netherfield, was he?"

"No, but he was not entirely welcoming either."

"I give up." Mary withdrew her head from the wardrobe. "I am worse than not very good at this. I am utterly lost."

Elizabeth joined Mary at the wardrobe. "What are you attempting to do? I thought you already had your gown chosen for tonight. You told me what you were wearing before you began working on your hair."

"This is not for me," Mary said in surprise. "This is for you. Tonight is the night to make Mr. Darcy regret his disparagement of you."

"And now you are sounding a great deal like Lydia."

Mary shrugged. "Lydia is not always wrong either."

"She is not?"

"Have you seen how many gentlemen fall over themselves to dance with her?"

Unfortunately, Elizabeth had.

"That is not just because she is lively," Mary continued. "She knows far too well how to display herself as a pretty package that every gentleman wishes were his."

"I do not want to be a pretty package. That sounds terribly wrong."

Mary chuckled. "Yes, you do want to be a pretty package. You just do not wish to be an inexpensive one. That is where Lydia goes wrong. She does not value herself highly enough."

Elizabeth grabbed Mary by the shoulders. "Please, could we go back to you not liking fashion or the idea of marrying before a lady is twenty-five?"

"I am not Mama. I will not push you toward Mr. Darcy, and I will not embarrass you. And I am not Lydia. I will not let you look tartish." She paused and a serious look settled onto her face. "You should look refined – dignified, but not stuffy. You could never be stuffy. I do not see how Mr. Darcy could not love you. I have always wished to be more like you."

"Me?" Elizabeth squeaked.

Mary nodded. "You may not be as beautiful as

Jane – few are – but you are enchanting." She shrugged. "People are drawn to you."

"Not Mr. Darcy."

"Maybe he is not yet drawn to you, but that can change, can it not? Just like I can change?"

As much as Elizabeth wished to say she doubted that Mr. Darcy would ever be drawn to her, she could not dash the hope that shimmered in Mary's eyes. If it helped her sister find her feet as who she wished to be, Elizabeth could pretend that she believed Mr. Darcy might eventually come to admire her. "It *is* nearly Christmas."

"And miracles are possible, are they not?" Mary asked hopefully.

Elizabeth nodded. "Especially at Christmas time."

Chapter 3

Despite Bingley's many reassurances that the Gardiners were quite genteel people, the home into which Darcy stepped was not at all like what he had expected. While the size of the hall and rooms were on a less grand scale than what he was used to, the fixtures and furnishings were of high quality. The décor was modern and understated. Nothing was garish, nor was anything in want of updating. Mr. Gardiner must be as Bingley said, wealthy, for no gentleman or lady kept a home's décor up to date without spending money.

"Welcome. Welcome. We are very pleased, even honoured, to have you join us for dinner tonight." A gentleman, who appeared to be only ten years older than Darcy and bearing a marked resemblance to Mrs. Bennet, greeted them. There was a liveliness to his expression that reminded Darcy in some way of his friend who was currently return-ing Mr. Gardiner's greeting.

"Charles Bingley." Bingley stuck out his hand and gave Mr. Gardiner's hand a firm shake. "It is a delight to meet you."

"The pleasure is mine. One can never have too many friends, I say."

Yes, the two men were much alike in Darcy mind.

"Speaking of friends, this is my friend, Mr. Fitzwilliam Darcy and his sister, Miss Darcy. Darcy, Georgiana, this is Mr. Gardiner and his wife, Mrs. Gardiner."

"Mr. Fitzwilliam Darcy," Mr. Gardiner said with a wide grin. "Now that is a name I have heard a time or two. My wife has told me many stories about your family."

"Has she?"

"Oh, yes, my Maddie likes to tell tales of her years in Lambton to the children. Now, as I under-stand it, the stories she tells were second-hand when she received them," he cautioned, "and I hope that there has not been too much distorting of the facts in the successive recitations."

"There often is some. It is only natural," Darcy

said. Of course, if the source of the stories were not favourably inclined to the individual about whom he spoke, that distortion would be great. However, since the Gardiners had invited him to their home, Darcy was going to believe that the stories which Mrs. Gardiner had heard were of the flattering sort.

"That is so true," Mrs. Gardiner said. "I do hope I have done your family justice in my relation of what I know. I have never heard a foul word about any of your relations," she added with a soft smile for Georgiana.

Whether the expression worked to make Georgiana feel at ease or not, as Darcy guessed it was designed to do, it had worked its magic on him as he had a challenging time not feeling some sort of affection for anyone who treated his sister well.

"I would expect nothing less," Darcy assured her.

Mrs. Gardiner was a young-looking lady. Her cheeks had not lost their bloom, and she had not one wrinkle or grey hair. Not that Darcy expected her to have such signs of age since, upon meeting her, he suspected that she was very nearly his age – perhaps only a year or two older. However, before meeting her, he had expected the possibility of such things from a lady who was an aunt to a lady of Elizabeth's age, for he had not expected to find that Miss Elizabeth's aunt and uncle were young. And, to be honest, it was a little unsettling.

"Please, be seated," Gardiner said with a flourish of his hand in the direction of the chairs and sofas of the room. "Oh!" he cried before they had moved more than two steps into the room. "Where are my manners? You would think I had never entertained before, and I assure you that I have and that I usually know my duty. However, it seems I have forgotten that your sister does not know my nieces."

Darcy had forgotten that as well in the warmth of his welcome. It was startling when he stopped to consider that he had, in such a short acquaintance, found himself feeling so at home as to forget an introduction.

"May I?" Mr. Gardiner directed the question to Darcy.

"Please."

"Miss Darcy," Mr. Gardiner said, "these two young ladies are just two of my five nieces. Miss Elizabeth Bennet."

Miss Elizabeth dipped a curtsey.

"And Miss Mary Bennet."

Darcy's eyes grew wide for the Miss Mary who curtseyed upon her introduction was not the severe-looking young woman he remembered from Hertfordshire. Her hair was soft, and she wore a gown with lace on it.

He was not usually the sort of gentleman to keep account of fashions worn by the ladies he met, but Miss Mary had appeared so austere whenever he had seen her in Hertfordshire, that it would have been more surprising for him to have not taken notice of her changed appearance than it was for him to remember what she had worn on former occasions when they had been in company together. She was, in his opinion, nearly as pretty as tonight her sister, Miss Elizabeth, who, he had to admit, was looking just as charming as she always did.

"I am delighted to meet you both," Georgiana said before leaving his side and going to sit with the Bennet sisters.

A smile curved Darcy's lips of its own accord. Apparently, Georgiana was feeling just as at ease as he was. While she had never been quite so reserved as he was, it was unusual for her to select a seat without following his lead. Once again, he was reminded that she was no longer a child but well on her way to becoming a gracious and confident lady, and if this were where she was going to find her confidence bolstered, then he was most happy to have it found here and in such a fashion. Miss Elizabeth would be a good friend for any young lady to have, and Miss Mary, well, she puzzled him. However, he knew she was not frivolous and flighty, so, for that reason, he supposed he could approve of her as a possible friend for his sister.

"You shall have to tell me about Netherfield," Georgiana was saying as Darcy took a seat. "I have heard so much about it from my brother that I find myself thinking I would like it quite well. However, he is a gentleman, and a gentleman does not always see things the same way we ladies do."

"Oh, you should visit," Miss Mary said.

"I would love to visit." She glanced at Darcy. "If my brother will allow it."

Darcy's smile faded. His sister seemed to be purposefully putting herself forward. "Georgiana," Darcy whispered. If this was the source of her apparent blossoming of confidence, he was not certain he approved after all.

"Maybe for Christmas?" Miss Mary suggested with a sidelong glance at Darcy.

Had the two young ladies been in communication with each other? No, that was impossible. Neither knew the other until just a moment ago. And yet, it seemed as if one knew exactly what the other was about.

"We are to return to Longbourn in time for Christmas," Mary added.

"We always spend Christmas in Hertfordshire," Mr. Gardiner inserted by way of explanation. "We spend a week at Longbourn and then, return to Gracechurch Street before Twelfth Night. However, that does not mean we miss out on any of the delights of the season on account of travelling, for we will begin our celebration tonight and it will not end until Twelfth Night." He smiled at his wife. "It is Madeline's favourite time of year."

"It is mine, too," Georgiana said.

"Is it indeed?" Mrs. Gardiner cried.

"My sister speaks the truth," Darcy assured her. "She is much like my mother was in that way."

"Oh," Mrs. Gardiner said on a sigh, "I have heard tales of the magnificent Christmas ball at Pemberley." She leaned forward as if telling a story or sharing a secret and lowered her voice to a level that begged to be heard. "It has been said that each year at Pemberley's Christmas ball some fortunate couple would fall in love for eternity."

Darcy chuckled. "My mother used to say the same thing, for it was at one of our grandmother's Christmas balls at Pemberley where she met our father."

"So it is true then?" Mrs. Gardiner could not keep the excitement from her voice. "I thought it was just my great aunt embellishing a tale for a girl who loved romantic notions."

"It was true for my parents," Darcy answered.

"And for my great aunt," Mrs. Gardiner added. "She was hired one year to help with the Christmas ball preparations." She looked to her nieces. "She was helping with the baking. She was always an excellent cook, even at the young age of fifteen."

She turned her attention back to Darcy. "There happened to be a groomsman from the stables who was sent to the kitchen to fetch some food for the arriving coachmen and groomsmen who were biding their time in the stables and having a bit of a party themselves."

She sighed. "My great aunt served him several

times that night. No matter if another man came up from the stables or not, whenever there was a need for anything from the house, that groomsman was also there. She said he must have travelled the distance from the stables to the house twelve times that night. And after that night, he travelled the distance from Pemberley's stables to Lambton so often as he was able to call on my great aunt until he finally found a position that allowed him the security to finally offer for her."

"Then, you are related to a former groomsman from Pemberley?" Bingley asked.

Mrs. Gardiner nodded. "In a roundabout way, I am. Though it is not a direct tie, I still claim it as an honour to have some link to such a wonderful home and lovely family." She paused. "I suppose a connection to a groomsman even from a place as beautiful as Pemberley is really not much to recommend me to most folks, especially in the finer sections of town, but in Lambton, it was something."

"It is such a wonderful story," Georgiana said. "I quite like that you have a connection to my home, do you not think so as well, Fitzwilliam?"

"I... I suppose I do," Darcy managed to answer.

Mr. Gardiner chuckled. "We gentlemen do not

get as..." He paused. "What is the word?" His brow furrowed. "I shall say it as we do not get as overcome with nostalgia as you ladies do. We are far less sentimental – no matter how hard we try to be more sentimental. It does not seem to be in our make up. Of course, I could be speaking out of turn, and it is only I who is such a fellow?" He looked first at Darcy and then Bingley.

"I would agree with you," Bingley answered. "And I know Darcy would, too." He chuckled. "He is perhaps the least romantic among us."

Darcy's ear burned.

"Practical sorts of fellows make excellent husbands and business owners," Mrs. Gardiner inserted. "Edward has improved, but he is still very much a numbers man and not a poet."

"But Maddie is determined to make our sons into poets," Mr. Gardiner added with a laugh.

"I might succeed with Albert."

"He is two," Mr. Gardiner said. "There is nothing practical about a two-year-old child. It is far too early to say if he will or will not be a poet. Now, back to Christmas. How will you all be spending it?"

"I intend to spend it at Netherfield," Bingley

said, "and perhaps a portion of it at Longbourn if I am fortunate."

"My mother would not hear of going the whole Yuletide season without having her neighbours visit," Miss Elizabeth said.

"Especially a neighbor with a good income and who is in want of a wife and whom our sister seems to favour," Mary added.

Darcy saw Miss Elizabeth's hand move to cover her sister's hand. The action was accompanied by a whispered scold.

"And you Mr. Darcy," Mr. Gardiner said. "How will you be spending Christmas?"

"We have not settled on that just yet." He gave his sister a pointed look when her lips parted as if she was going to speak.

"Well, if you are remaining in town, Maddie and I would be delighted to include you and your sister in our Christmas here in Gracechurch Street."

"Oh, may we?" Georgiana asked eagerly.

Darcy looked from her to the ladies on the sofa next to her and then to Mrs. Gardiner and her husband. Four of those five people seemed hopeful that he would agree.

"We would not wish to intrude on a special family time," he said.

"You would not be," Mr. Gardiner assured him. "You are invited to join us, and we would all be delighted to have you."

Darcy cast one more look in Elizabeth's direction. He was not certain she was so delighted as her uncle seemed to think she was. "If you are certain..."

Elizabeth's eyes met his, and the left side of her lips curved up into a small almost-welcoming half-smile. It was enough to make his heart thump a little harder, which in turn shouted to him that what he was about to say was a mistake. However, his mouth was just as incapable of helping him escape his current situation as his plan to leave Netherfield had been.

"I think we can be persuaded to take part in, at least, some of the festivities of Christmas at Gracechurch Street."

Chapter 4

"We do not do this each night until Christmas," Mr. Gardiner said as he settled back in his chair at the top of the dining table at the conclusion of their meal, "but the first night that we mark in our celebration must be special."

Elizabeth watched Mr. Darcy's expression carefully. She had been observing him all evening, and she had not seen him scowl in disapproval or arch a critical eyebrow since he arrived, save for twice – once, when his sister had mentioned going to Netherfield and again, when he had been asked to take part in the festivities at Gracechurch Street. She would dearly love to know why those two things had caused his features to briefly darken with discomfort. Was it because he found both the society of Hertfordshire and here, at her aunt and uncle's home, to be too lowly for his sister and himself? Or was it something else?

She had wanted to put it to simple arrogance, and she had tried. However, the way in which he had greeted her two young cousins as if they were people of importance had made her doubt that it was superiority which had made him uneasy.

"Your cook has done an excellent job of making our meal a feast of celebration," Mr. Darcy said with a smile that appeared to Elizabeth to be genuine and not affected. "I have not had such delicious rabbit pie in an age, and I shall have to request that my cook presents it in such an enchanting fashion, as it was tonight, the next time it is served."

"You have never had it served in the form of a beggar's purse?" Elizabeth asked. She had been almost positive that he would find their meal wanting in some way. Or maybe she was just hoping that he would so that she would have another reason, other than his comment at the assembly, to dislike him. It was truly disappointing that he was being all that was pleasant – even if he was doing it in a reserved fashion.

"It is a present," Martin corrected.

Elizabeth shifted her gaze from Mr. Darcy to the eldest Gardiner child who sat across from her and next to his mother. "My apologies, Martin."

She turned her focus back to Mr. Darcy, who sat at the top of the table next to her uncle and across from Mr. Bingley. "Have you never had rabbit pie in the form of a present, Mr. Darcy?"

His lips twitched in amusement. "No, I have not."

Was he laughing at her? Or did he find Martin's insistence on the correct term being *present* to be humorous?

"Good food is an indulgence which I cannot deny myself," Mr. Gardiner interjected before Elizabeth could decipher the source of Mr. Darcy's amusement. "Therefore, an excellent cook is required, and we treat him well."

Mr. Bingley chuckled. "As you should! An excellent cook should never be treated in any other way than well since they can be a trial to find."

"Indeed," Mr. Darcy agreed. "Netherfield also has an excellent cook, as does Longbourn." He glanced for a fleeting minute in Elizabeth's direction.

"I have not sampled any of the delights of

Netherfield, but I have eaten at Longbourn many times and would have to agree. Both of my sisters are very accomplished when it comes to entertaining guests, and an accomplished cook is paramount to such enterprises." Mr. Gardiner lowered his voice. "Do not tell either of them this, but Mrs. Bennet is perhaps better than Mrs. Philips. I cannot hope to do so well as either of them." Mr. Gardiner laughed. "However, Maddy can outshine them both." He winked at his wife, who smiled and shook her head.

Aunt Gardiner was fond of her husband's praise, but she often scolded him for it because, according to her, she only did what needed to be done for her family in the best way she knew how to do it. It is what any good wife should do, she would say. To which, Uncle Gardiner would always reply that commending his wife on her excellence was what any good husband should do. Elizabeth hoped that she would be so fortunate as to marry a gentleman like her uncle who did not hide his admiration of his wife.

"I hope you will not be put out if we do not have our dessert course now," Mrs. Gardiner said. "The children do better with some time between their main meal and any sweets."

"I think that is an excellent plan," Mr. Darcy assured her.

He was being exceptionally friendly and agreeable this evening. Elizabeth tipped her head and studied his handsome profile. She supposed he had always been polite – well, except for that time at the assembly when he said that horrid thing he said. She sighed. Perhaps it was just her that he did not like, which meant, of course, that there was no hope of him ever considering her.

"We have promised the children a game and a story before they can have their Christmas wafers and a touch of tea," Mr. Gardiner said.

"A game?"

Elizabeth smiled. That was a third time that Mr. Darcy had looked apprehensive this evening.

"Which game?" Mr. Bingley asked eagerly, looking down the table to the Gardiner children.

"*Hunt the Slipper*," Nora said. Her eyes twinkled in the candlelight, and her cheeks were rosy. Five-year-old Nora loved to play games. She was not so good, however, at losing games.

"And whose slipper shall we use?" Mr. Bingley questioned her. "Mine?"

The little girl giggled and shook her head.

"Mr. Darcy's?"

Elizabeth could not help but join her cousin in giggling at such an absurd suggestion. Mr. Bingley was very amusing. Jane would do well to have him as her husband. Her children would never want for entertainment.

"I do suppose his slippers would be too big to hide," Mr. Bingley gave Mr. Darcy a teasing grin.

A quick peek at Mr. Darcy could not be helped. Elizabeth simply had to see how he would respond. His left eyebrow arched, and he gave his friend a withering look.

"They are not that much larger than yours," he said in defense of himself.

Surprisingly, when Elizabeth turned her eyes back to Mr. Bingley, he looked pleased with himself for having drawn such a response from his friend. The sight went against everything she had thought of Mr. Bingley before. Hopefully, he was not the sort to provoke others for sport.

"Mine," Nora said. "Papa said we could use mine."

"That I did," Mr. Gardiner agreed.

"Then, yours it shall be, Miss Gardiner," Mr. Bingley said.

"Shall we go to the sitting room?" Mrs. Gardiner asked.

"Oh, yes!" Martin cried.

Six-year-old Martin also loved a good game, and he was particularly good at winning them. His trial with playing games came in the form of an inability to be a humble winner, which did little to aid his younger sister with her struggle in losing graciously. Perhaps tonight, they would be fortunate and someone other than Martin would win.

It did not take long at all to walk the few steps from the dining room to the sitting room. While her aunt and uncle's home was spacious enough for their growing family and any guests they might have visit, it was not sprawling. The corridor was narrower than Longbourn's, and there were fewer rooms on each level of the townhouse.

"You must sit in a circle on the floor," Martin instructed once everyone had entered the sitting room. That was another thing at which Martin excelled – telling others what needed to be done.

"Try again," Mrs. Gardiner said with a pointed

look for her eldest. "But this time, request that we join you rather than demanding it."

Mr. Darcy's lips twitched with amusement again. While the response to a child being reprimanded was odd to Elizabeth, the affect amusement had in softening Mr. Darcy's features was appealing. She sighed. If only she were more than tolerable.

"You must sit by Mr. Darcy," Mary hissed in Elizabeth's ear.

Elizabeth shook her head.

"You must," Mary mouthed without sound. "Please."

"I would be quite pleased if you would sit on the floor in a circle," Martin said.

"Better," his mother assured him when he looked to her for approval.

"Who will stand in the middle first?" Mr. Bingley asked as he sat down.

"Martin because he is the oldest," Nora said as she took a place next to Mr. Bingley. To Elizabeth, it looked as if the slightly silly Mr. Bingley had found an admirer.

"Is it not the youngest who goes first?" Mr. Bingley asked.

"No," Nora answered simply.

"My sister, Caroline, always said it was," Mr. Bingley replied.

"It is not." Nora's expression was all seriousness.

"We need your slipper," Martin said to his sister.

"Try again," his mother said.

"May I have your slipper, please?"

"Better."

For a third time since the end of dinner, Mr. Darcy's lips twitched with amusement. If he was laughing at a child being corrected... well... that was not something which Elizabeth could condone.

"At the risk of being far too impertinent," she whispered, as she took a seat next to Mr. Darcy to please her sister, "may I ask what is so humorous about a child being scolded?"

His eyes grew wide. "My apologies. I was not laughing at your cousin."

He looked disquieted enough that Elizabeth had to believe him.

"I was simply remembering how often either I or one of my two older cousins had to repeat things more politely when we were younger." He turned his attention back to Martin with a pensive look on his face.

The thought of a young Mr. Darcy being reprimanded for his behaviour by his mother made her smile before it cast a shadow of melancholy on her. She glanced at the gentleman sitting next to her. He had neither mother nor father. Had it been his mother who had reprimanded him? Or was it his father? Who was he remembering?

"Did it happen often?" she asked.

He nodded. "Far more often than it should have." His lips curled up into a small smile. "Much to my shame, I have not outgrown that fault. However, I rarely have anyone who scolds me for poor behaviour now."

"Cobbler, cobbler mend my shoe..."

Mr. Darcy and Elizabeth turned their attention back to the game just as Martin handed the slipper to Mr. Bingley and closed his eyes. As quickly and quietly as possible, the slipper passed from hand to hand behind each person's back.

For half an hour, laughter and fun filled the Gardiner sitting room as Nora's slipper was hidden and then hunted. Several got to take their turns standing in the middle of the group trying to find the slipper, though anyone taller than Martin was required to stand on his or her knees so they could not look over the heads of the slipper passers.

"And now for a story!" Mr. Gardiner cried once Nora's slipper had been returned to her foot and all had claimed a seat on the furniture instead of the floor. "What story shall it be, Nora?"

Nora clapped her hands. "I get to choose?"

"You do, indeed," her father replied.

"The one about the landlord and Fanny."[1]

"She always picks that one," Martin grumbled.

"Not always," Nora retorted.

"Almost," Martin replied.

"Children," their father interrupted, "go sit by your mother." He waited until he saw that both his children had obeyed before turning back to his guests. "This story will require some help for it is a bit of a play."

Elizabeth pressed her lips together so that she would not laugh at the look of sheer horror that washed over Mr. Darcy's face before it could be hidden.

"Who reads the best among you?" Mr. Gardiner continued. "I know that Elizabeth and Mary are both excellent readers."

"I will be Betty," Mary offered eagerly, "and Elizabeth can be Fanny."

"Gentlemen, do you read?" Mr. Gardiner posed the question to Mr. Bingley and Mr. Darcy.

"Darcy is the better reader," Mr. Bingley answered.

"You are more expressive," Mr. Darcy said with a shake of his head.

Mr. Gardiner chuckled. "Reluctant performers, are we? Then, I shall play the landlord, and," he scanned the story he held, "Mr. Bingley can be John – he is the farmer – and Mr. Darcy will play Thomas – the farmer's son. The parts are nearly the same length. Will that suit?"

"Yes," Mary answered with alacrity and a smile for Elizabeth.

Dread settled in Elizabeth's stomach as her uncle gave instructions for Mary and Elizabeth to share one copy of the story while Mr. Darcy and Mr. Bingley shared another. Swiftly, the sitting room was rearranged to have a gallery of observers – consisting of Mrs. Gardiner, her two eldest children, and Miss Darcy – and a performance area with one chair in the middle and two sets of two chairs on either side of the central chair.

"Is this not perfect?" Mary whispered to Elizabeth after they had taken their places on the right side of their uncle and Mr. Darcy and Mr. Bingley had been seated on Mr. Gardiner's left. "Perhaps playing the part of a gentleman in love with you will be just the thing."

"No, it is not perfect," Elizabeth hissed. She had no desire to read the part of Fanny, the orphan girl who was promised to the farmer's son.

"It is Providence," Mary whispered happily. "Providence and a bit of Yuletide magic."

"I do not think the Good Lord uses magic at any time of the year," Elizabeth grumbled.

"No, of course, He does not," Mary said with a wave of her hand, "but you know what I mean."

"You are sounding like Lydia," Elizabeth cautioned.

Mary batted her lashes. "I intended to."

As her uncle stood to welcome their audience, Elizabeth sighed and wished for the old Mary to return just until Mr. Darcy had departed for the evening. Then, she prepared herself to read her part and declare her determination to join her lot as Fanny with Mr. Darcy's as Thomas.

Notes

1. The Landlord's Visit from Evenings at Home; Or, The Juvenile Budget Opened, Consisting of a Variety of Miscellaneous Pieces, for the Instruction and Amusement of Young Persons by John Aikin (1793)

Chapter 5

Shopping. Darcy shook his head. How had he once again been relegated to chaperoning his sister while she visited more shops?

"Thank you for allowing your sister to accompany Mary and me today."

That was how. The intoxicating lady on his arm was the sole reason he had agreed to take part in yet another shopping excursion. She had haunted his dreams as the play, of which they had been a part, played out in mind the past two nights.

"It is Mary's first visit to London without our parents," Miss Elizabeth explained in hushed tones as they walked behind Miss Mary and Georgiana. "She is quite enthusiastic about enjoying all that town has to offer her, or, at least, all that she will be allowed to enjoy." There was a hint of a laugh in Miss Elizabeth's tone.

"She seems," he paused, "different."

Miss Elizabeth grimaced. "She is."

They walked on in silence as he waited for her to say more. However, that was the length and breadth of her reply, and it did nothing to ease his confusion about the Miss Mary Bennet he had met two nights ago at the Gardiners.

"Georgiana seems to like her." Perhaps that would prompt Miss Elizabeth to share more information.

"She does." Again, the brief reply did nothing to help him determine who this new Bennet sister was.

Just then, Georgiana peeked over her shoulder at him with something a lot like mischief in her expression. The sight was a bit unnerving.

He glanced nonchalantly to his right and then his left. They were removed enough from anyone who might be gathering gossip about what he was doing. If Miss Elizabeth was not going to be forthcoming with information in a casual conversation, perhaps he needed to try a different approach to the topic.

"I must confess that I am uncertain if I should encourage their friendship or not."

He felt the hand which lay on his arm flinch before Miss Elizabeth slowly withdrew it.

"Can you not help me decide?" he asked.

Miss Elizabeth fidgeted with her gloves as if ensuring they were securely on her hands. "Why do you think the friendship should not be encouraged?"

They had stopped walking in front of a shop while Miss Mary and Georgiana were admiring the items on display in the window. Taking note that both Miss Annesley and John, the footman who had once again accompanied them on a shopping excursion, were attending to the two young ladies, Darcy turned his attention back to Miss Elizabeth. The expression on her face seemed to say that his answer was of great importance. Therefore, he weighed his words carefully before speaking.

"I do not know your sister. I thought I had some understanding of who she was, but," he shook his head, "she is so different."

"Lizzy," Miss Mary called with a wave of her hand beckoning her sister forward. "Do you see the edge of the lace the clerk is displaying to that woman?" she asked once Miss Elizabeth had joined her.

Miss Elizabeth peered through the window.

"Would not Mama love it?" Miss Mary asked.

"I am certain she would."

"Shall we get it for her?"

Miss Elizabeth hesitated before answering. "If it is not too dear, but remember, there is also the book for Papa's gift that we must purchase."

"But you are happy with the lace as a present for Mama?"

Miss Elizabeth nodded and smiled. "Delighted." She turned back to Darcy. "We would like to enter this shop, sir."

"You may enter whichever shops you would like."

His sister pressed her lips together as if she wished to laugh. Then, as Miss Mary and Miss Elizabeth went into the store together, Georgiana wrapped her arm around his.

"Do you not simply adore the Miss Bennets, Fitzwilliam?"

"They are very pleasant company," he answered carefully.

"Are they both *just* pleasant company?"

"Yes, what else would they be?"

She shrugged. "Oh, I do not know." She drew

him toward a display case. "Did you know that Miss Elizabeth's favourite fragrance is lavender?" she asked as she bent down to look more closely at the gloves in the case.

Heat began to creep up Darcy's neck. "No, I did not know." Although, he could have guessed it was because she wore the fragrance so frequently. In fact, she was wearing it today. "And does Miss Mary have a favourite fragrance?"

Georgiana nodded. "Roses. It is too bad I purchased those gloves the other day. These are beautiful."

"Do you wish for another pair?"

She shook her head. "No, I have enough pairs for now, but what do you think of these – for yourself?" She pointed to a fine pair of black leather gloves.

"They appear to be of good quality." And his were showing their wear.

"They do," his sister agreed.

He motioned for the clerk for assistance. "This pair, please."

"Whatever fragrance Miss Elizabeth is wearing today smells a lot like my new one. Do you not think so?"

Darcy turned the pair of gloves over in his hand, paying close attention to the seaming and purpose-fully refraining from looking at his sister. "I really could not say," or more precisely he would not say. He did, in fact, know that the two fragrances were similar. "Why do you ask?" He finally looked at her after informing the clerk he would take the gloves.

"Mere curiosity." Her eyes held his. "Your ears are red. Are you cold?" Then, she turned away with a smile before he could reply.

Her observation made his ears grow warmer.

"I actually find it rather warm in here," he grum-bled, fully unwilling to admit that his red ears had anything to do with their conversation. "This is just part of the trouble with shopping. You dress for the weather so you can abide the out of doors, but then, when you enter a shop you become over-heated. I am certain that many illnesses start just this way."

Georgiana's shoulders shook as she laughed silently. "You sound like Aunt Catherine when she is complaining about drafts," she finally said when she had stopped laughing. "Are you prepared to rejoin the frigid weather outside, Fitzwilliam? For it appears Miss Mary and Miss Elizabeth have secured their purchase, which I am certain you know since you are watching them."

"I am responsible for all of you. I must watch them, as well as you." Impertinence in Miss Elizabeth was far more becoming than it was in his sister.

"Oh, yes, of course."

Her words agreed with him completely, but her amused tone did nothing of the sort.

"Shall we?" he motioned to the door.

"I want to walk with Miss Mary when she reaches the street."

"Very well."

"Did you know that she is just two years, three months, and five days older than me?"

"No."

"Did you know her youngest sister is just four months and two days older than me?"

"I knew you and Miss Lydia were close in age, but I did not know how close."

"Miss Mary plays the piano."

"That I did know." Not that he found her playing to be the sort that he preferred to listen to. She was accurate, but there was no emotion.

"Could we visit the sweets shop, and after, go to

Darcy House for tea early? Then, I could show her my new book of music."

"Their aunt will not be there until the prescribed time."

Mrs. Gardiner had been delighted to give her permission for her nieces to be escorted from shop to shop by Mr. Darcy because she had some tasks she had hoped to accomplish today and the extra time to complete them was most welcome. However, she had been adamant that she would join them for tea. She would not expect Mrs. Annesley to be the sole chaperone for three young ladies in a single gentleman's home – not even if one of those young ladies was the gentleman's sister.

Georgiana sighed. "Then, we will have to visit the booksellers next."

"I do not mind that shop at all." In fact, it was one of his favourites.

"Which shop is that?" Miss Mary asked as she joined them.

"The bookseller's shop," Georgiana answered. "It is the only shop where Fitzwilliam could spend a full day and not complain about it."

"That is true," Darcy agreed. "Though I do prefer spending a day in my library since the books there have already been purchased."

"It is Lizzy's favourite shop, as well as Papa's," Mary inserted.

"I like books," Elizabeth said defensively.

"So do we," Mary argued back.

Apparently, Miss Mary already knew that Darcy was not the only member of his family who liked to read.

"Then, it sounds like it will be an excellent place for us all to be," Mrs. Annesley inserted.

"Do you like books, too?" Miss Mary asked Georgiana's companion.

"Since before I could read for myself." She neatly turned Miss Mary and Georgiana in the direction they needed to go. She seemed just as good as she appeared upon his first meeting her. There was not even a hint of anything improper in this companion – unlike Mrs. Young, Georgiana's former companion.

"They have left us together again." He offered Miss Elizabeth his arm.

"So I noticed." She placed her hand on his arm. "They truly do seem perfectly matched as friends, do they not?"

He watched his sister lean towards Miss Mary and whisper something that caused them both to giggle. Georgiana did not usually make friends so easily as she seemed to have done with Miss Mary.

"They do," he admitted.

"Will you allow the friendship to continue?"

He glanced at her. Georgiana being friends with Miss Mary would make it much harder for him to avoid Miss Elizabeth.

"Please?" Miss Elizabeth added.

"I believe I can do that since I have already gained your assurance that your sister poses no danger to mine." Though he was still curious about the change in Miss Mary.

Relief washed over Miss Elizabeth's face as she thanked him.

"Mr. Darcy! Miss Darcy!"

Darcy cringed at the sound of his name falling from Miss Bingley's lips.

"And Miss Mary and Miss Elizabeth, too?" Mrs. Hurst added. "What a cozy group you all make."

"Miss Bingley, Mrs. Hurst." Darcy gave a nod of his head in greeting. "Is Bingley with you?"

"No," Miss Bingley gave Elizabeth an appraising look. "Charles refused to join us because he says he has some business to finish before he returns to Netherfield, but Louisa and I just could not wait for him to do whatever it is he needs to do. There are far too many details which must be seen to before the season begins."

"Mr. Darcy will know about that soon enough, Caroline. It is just one more year before you are out, is it not, Miss Darcy?" Mrs. Hurst asked.

"As you know," Darcy answered.

"We would be happy to help her prepare," Mrs. Hurst added.

"My aunt has already claimed that duty."

Mrs. Hurst's hopeful expression slid into disappointment for a moment before it brightened again. "I am certain there can be no one better than Lady Matlock to assist a young lady. She is highly respected."

"And she has such good taste," Miss Bingley agreed. "Not at all like some who parade themselves around the season." Again, her eyes flicked to Miss Elizabeth with an assessing look.

Mrs. Hurst tittered as she agreed with her sister.

"You will have to visit us now that we are back in town," Miss Bingley said to Georgiana. "And you, too, of course, Miss Elizabeth and Miss Mary," she added belatedly.

"That will be up to our aunt," Miss Mary inserted. "We are under her care while we are in town."

"Do you mean your relations in Cheapside?" Mrs. Hurst asked.

"Near Cheapside," Darcy corrected. "In Gracechurch Street."

"Oh, forgive me." Mrs. Hurst gave him a quizzical look. "Have you met them?"

He nodded. "Georgiana and I had dinner with them two nights ago."

"Oh." She looked from him to Miss Elizabeth. "How kind of you."

"Excessively," Miss Elizabeth agreed.

"We must be on our way," Darcy said. "We are expecting Mrs. Gardiner to join us for tea shortly."

"At Darcy House?"

Had he ever seen Miss Bingley's eyes grow so wide?

"Yes, at Darcy House. If you will excuse us, we have another shop to visit before we return home." He gave a nod of his head and left them.

"I do not understand it," Georgiana said once

they were away from Miss Bingley and Mrs. Hurst. "Caroline is usually more friendly than that."

"Not always," Darcy said. "You have not seen her at soirees during the season."

"Or in Hertfordshire." He heard Miss Mary mutter.

"Was she rude there, too?" Georgiana whispered.

Miss Mary nodded.

It was a small movement, but it carried a powerful blow. If Miss Mary found Miss Bingley's behaviour to be wanting, then, she must have also found his to be in need of improvement, for he had behaved just as poorly. Disappointment with himself settled into his stomach like a heavy rock just as it had always done when his mother had scolded him for poor behaviour. However, unlike when he was young, he could not just redo what he had done improperly... or could he?

Chapter 6

Of all the Lydia-like things for Mary to do! Elizabeth tamped down her annoyance at her sister's obvious attempt at matchmaking and determined she would have a pointed discussion with the new version of Mary when they arrived back at Gracechurch Street. For now, she would play along with the ploy that Mary and Miss Darcy wanted to look through the magazine which had been purchased at the bookseller's shop. If her sister's eyes had stayed on the fashion plates instead of peeking up with a smile at Elizabeth, Elizabeth might have believed that Mary was genuinely interested in the magazine she and Georgians held between them.

"Oh, look at this one!" Miss Darcy cried. "I think you would look beautiful in it."

"Do you truly think so? I have never worn that colour before."

"I think you have the perfect coloring for it," Miss Darcy assured her.

Even though she was annoyed with her sister, Elizabeth could not help but smile at how lovely it was to see Mary making a friend and enjoying that friend's companionship. It made her feel as if a wrong was being corrected. The wrong being, of course, Elizabeth's inattention to her sister before now. She had always just assumed Mary was happy with her solitary existence until two days ago when she admitted to being lonely.

Elizabeth cast a glance at her bench mate, who happened to be Miss Darcy's doting older brother. A small smile tipped his lips and softened his expression. She had not thought that Mr. Darcy would be such a generous and loving brother. However, from everything she had seen today, it was true, and his sister did not seem spoiled or ill-tempered because of it. Indeed, she seemed a sensible girl despite her obvious youthfulness and innocence. A lady could easily find herself enamoured with such a gentleman.

Oh, Mary needed to stop pushing her towards Mr. Darcy! Walking from store to store on his arm had been wonderful, and sitting here beside him now, as they travelled to Darcy House, was delightful. However, such pleasures made it nearly impossible for her to continue to dislike him, and when her anger and displeasure faded, there was only the sting of his words and the pain of his rejection to fill the void. Again, Elizabeth told herself that a pointed discussion of these things would need to be had with Mary.

"We are nearly there." Mr. Darcy interrupted Elizabeth's thoughts about him and turned them only the smallest amount.

This was his neighbourhood? She studied the buildings more carefully, eager to discover all there was to know about him even while she told herself that doing so was foolish. As she looked out the window at the rows of homes that lined the street, she no longer wondered at Miss Bingley scoffing at Meryton. These homes were magnificent – far grander than Elizabeth had ever imagined. She had known that they would be finer than her aunt and uncle's home, but the size of some of them!

"The area is lovely," she said, turning to Darcy.

"I like it," Mr. Darcy replied with a smile.

She pulled her eyes away from his beautiful smile and once again attended to the houses outside the carriage window. "It would be a strange thing indeed if you did not, sir," she teased.

Mr. Darcy chuckled. She liked it when he did that. She liked it far too much, for it was nearly as heart-fluttering as his smile was, and, when he chuckled, she did not have to be facing him to enjoy it. But she should not enjoy it. He did not like her, and if things continued to progress down this path of admiration for the gentleman beside her, the one Christmas gift she would be taking back to Longbourn for herself would be a broken heart, completely and utterly of her own doing.

"I suppose it would," he agreed.

The carriage began to slow in front of what appeared to be the largest home on the street. Elizabeth's lashes fluttered over wide eyes. "This is Darcy House?"

In her mind, she had known that ten thousand a year was a fortune and that Mr. Darcy was wealthy. But she had not imagined just how wealthy he must be until at this moment as she gazed upon his house.

Mr. Darcy nodded. "This is home when we are in town."

This house was not just grand. It was astonishing so. She turned her eyes toward him. He was looking out the window and wearing the most peaceful smile which told her in clear terms that the word *home* was more than the name of an object. It was a place where he found comfort.

"It is enormous," Mary muttered, and Elizabeth nodded her agreement.

"It is spacious," Darcy conceded.

"But it is not cold," Miss Darcy added. "It is warm and welcoming, is it not, Fitzwilliam?"

"I find it so," he replied.

The carriage door opened, and the steps were put in place. Darcy was the first to exit the carriage, followed by Miss Darcy.

"Miss Mary," Darcy held his hand out to help her from the carriage, and then, once Mary was standing next to Miss Darcy, he provided the same service to Elizabeth. However, he did not relinquish her hand once her feet were on the ground as he had Mary's. No, he did not release it at all. Instead, he tucked it in the crook of his elbow and led her ahead of his sister and hers toward the massive black door to the house.

"Welcome to Darcy House," he said when they

had stepped through the doorway into the entrance hall.

There was a marked note of pride in his voice, and why would there not be? His home was beautiful. Every house, in which Elizabeth had ever been, paled in comparison to the elegance of the décor here. The mouldings, the marble floor, the table under the mirror, the chairs that stood next to the staircase, the paintings that hung on the walls of the gallery above her – they were all exquisite.

"Has Mrs. Gardiner arrived yet, Beggs?"

"Yes, sir. I have put her in the green drawing room."

"Are the refreshments on their way?"

"As soon as Tom reaches the kitchen, sir."

Another one of Mr. Darcy's beautiful smiles accompanied his nod of approval. It appeared he was not only a doting brother but also a kind employer.

"Miss Elizabeth." He offered her his arm.

She only hesitated a moment before returning her hand to his arm. It was becoming a familiar feeling to be walking so close to him for she had done it so often today. However, she had to admit it did feel somewhat more significant to be doing so here, in his home, as he led them all up the grand staircase to the first floor and down the gallery to what was, according to Mr. Beggs, the green drawing room.

"Mrs. Gardiner, I have returned your nieces safely to you, though I do believe their purses might be lighter than they were."

"I hope that their money was spent wisely." Aunt Gardiner's eyes held a question when she shifted her gaze from Mr. Darcy to Elizabeth.

"We purchased two gifts." Elizabeth removed her hand from Mr. Darcy's arm. "Some lace for Mama, and a book for Papa."

"Please be seated," Darcy inserted.

Elizabeth breathed a sigh of relief and crossed to where her aunt was sitting. As much as she enjoyed being at Mr. Darcy's side, she did not revel in the curious look in her aunt's eye.

"Was it an enjoyable shopping excursion?" Mrs. Gardiner asked Mary.

"Very," Mary answered with alacrity and a smile for Elizabeth. "I have never enjoyed shopping more."

Mrs. Gardiner laughed. "You will have to come to town more often."

"May I?" Mary's expression was suffused with joy.

"I think you are a good age to begin coming to town more often." Mrs. Gardiner sighed softly. "We have yet to be successful in introducing one of your sisters to a promising suitor, but that does not mean we cannot try to do the same for you."

"Indeed?"

Elizabeth was almost certain that Mary would have danced a jig if she had not been in the green drawing room at Darcy House. Her delight was palpable.

"I dare say we will not have Jane to think of much longer," Mrs. Gardiner said, as Mary took a seat next to Miss Darcy. "Forgive me, Mr. Darcy. I promise you that I do not speak of making matches often. Indeed, it is only when we are so close to the season, when Jane and, sometimes, Elizabeth come to visit, that my mind becomes overrun with such thoughts. Not that I do not have them at other times, of course, but the season brings them to the fore."

"Do you take part in the season?" Miss Darcy asked Elizabeth.

"No. At least, not as you think of it." She hoped

that such a reply would be the end of that dis-cussion. The sooner the topic of conversation was turned away from all things related to finding a husband, the happier Elizabeth would be.

"How do you take part in it?" Mr. Darcy, the reason for Elizabeth wishing to not discuss things related to courting and marrying, asked.

"We do as we always do when in town. My aunt and uncle enjoy hosting dinner parties, and we take in some of the amusements that town has to offer." Elizabeth looked at her aunt. How was she supposed to say that there were more eligible gen-tlemen in town during the season than at other times without sounding as if she was hunting for a husband? She certainly did not want Mr. Darcy to think she was considering him.

"Due to the greater population, the amusements and availability of dinner guests increases," Mrs. Gardiner elaborated. "My husband is not without his connections, and, as would be suspected, some of those are connections to wealthy tradesmen, but there are also gentlemen of his acquaintance who own solvent estates and who only come to town during the season."

Mr. Darcy nodded his understanding. "That is

very like how it is during the season amongst the ton as well."

"My aunt and uncle put themselves out more while Jane and I are with them, and for that, we are grateful, especially since Meryton is lacking in some of what town can provide." Elizabeth could feel her cheeks growing warm.

"I am not certain I understand," Miss Darcy said softly.

"There are not very many marriageable gentlemen in Meryton," Mary said plainly.

"Oh. Well. Yes. That would make it challenging to find a husband, would it not?" Mr. Darcy said.

"Very much so," Mary agreed. "I assure you that it caused quite the stir when Mr. Bingley arrived in the area."

"Mary," Elizabeth chided softly with a pointed glance toward Mr. Darcy.

Mary pressed her lips together, and Elizabeth hoped the topic of gentlemen and marrying would die a natural death. However, her hopes were to be dashed.

"May I be so bold as to be inquisitive?" Mr. Darcy began, drawing Elizabeth's attention along with everyone else's.

Mr. Darcy had his elbows on the arm of his chair. His hands, though clasped together in front of him in what one might consider a casual fashion, flexed into a tight closure and then relaxed before repeating the same motion again and again. Was he nervous? Elizabeth looked up to his face. There was a marked uneasiness in his features that made her wonder if being inquisitive was something he was not very often.

"Of course, you may," Mrs. Gardiner replied.

"Is the lack of gentlemen in Meryton why you were not dancing at the assembly?" He directed the question to Elizabeth. "When I first saw you, you were not dancing," he added when Elizabeth did not immediately answer.

She had not answered both because the question took her by surprise and because she would rather not discuss that particular assembly with him. However, it would be rude to not say something.

"Yes, it was not because I was slighted by other gentlemen." His words rang in her ears as she said it, and she once again felt the stab of mortification she had felt at first hearing them.

Her reply caused Mr. Darcy's eyes to widen as if

startled, and embarrassment coloured his features. Had he not realized she had heard his comment? He had looked right at her, had he not?

"I wondered afterward why you were not dancing," he said and then fell silent.

Afterward? Did he mean after his comment about her being merely tolerable and slighted by other gentlemen? Or did he mean after the ball was over? Either way, it was startling to hear that he had been thinking about her when she was not present.

"Are balls as fun as I imagine them to be?" Miss Darcy asked Mary.

Elizabeth was thankful for the turn in the conversation.

"Do you like dancing?" Mary answered.

"Oh, yes. I do when my feet can remember the steps."

"Then," Mary continued, "I suppose balls are just as pleasurable as you imagine them to be."

It was an impressively wise reply. Elizabeth darted a cautious look toward Mr. Darcy and hoped such a reply helped ease his mind further about Mary's friendship with Miss Darcy.

"It is the speaking to my partner while remembering my steps part which has me most anxious," Miss Darcy admitted.

"Some partners are better than other at helping with that," Mary assured her.

"You need a list of topics," Mrs. Gardiner interjected. "Things about which it is easy to converse such as the weather, the décor of the room, the season of the year, or the colour of a dress. Having such a list prepared beforehand can be a handy thing to help settle the nerves," Mrs. Gardiner added. "I should not admit it since she is not here, but Jane had the same worry when she was about your age. Such a list has always helped her."

"Jane?" Mary asked in surprise.

Mrs. Gardiner nodded. "She is very good at appearing to be sure of herself when she is not, and I am certain, she is not the only young woman to ever feel so." She glanced at Elizabeth.

"Oh, I am sure she is not," Elizabeth agreed before anyone could guess that her aunt was hinting that she had also been given that same list of things about which to speak when she was preparing for her first assembly. Of course, she was not so reserved as Jane; therefore, she had had fewer trepidations. Yet, still, there had been some nerves.

Those nerves had been vanquished by her success at her first ball and had remained in exile until Mr. Darcy had entered the assembly rooms in Meryton. Now, they seemed to think they could become her dear companions.

"A list is a very good idea," Mr. Darcy said as trays of tea and sweets were brought in and a table was set up for them. "I will have to remember that trick."

"You?" The moment the word left her mouth, Elizabeth wished to suck it back in.

Mr. Darcy nodded in reply as he rose to go to the tea-table. "I do not excel at conversing with strangers," he said to her before adding, "Georgiana, if you would help me, please."

He was going to serve the tea? Elizabeth snapped her mouth closed. Did they not have a maid who could do it? The maid standing near watche with wide eyes. Apparently, she found the situation just as unusual as Elizabeth did.

"For Miss Elizabeth," he said, handing a cup to his sister, who carried it to Elizabeth. "How do you like your tea, Mrs. Gardiner?"

"As it comes from the pot," she answered.

Elizabeth took a sip of the tea in her cup. It was

prepared just how she liked it – with a bit of milk and a touch of sweetness. Her eyes met Mr. Darcy's. Had he been watching her?

"Did I remember correctly?" he asked.

"Perfectly."

His lips tipped up into the most adorable, satisfied smile before he turned to Mary to see how she liked her tea.

He had remembered how she took her tea. How extraordinary! Was it from when she was at Netherfield?

"Would you care for a Banbury cake?" He had finished serving the tea and was now before her with a plate on which was an oval pastry, hiding currants and spices between its layers of paste.

"I am sure I could never refuse a Banbury cake," she replied lightly.

"I thought as much. You seemed to enjoy them when you were at Netherfield."

Her heart skittered. Not only had he remembered how she took her tea, but he had also noticed which sweet she preferred during her stay at Netherfield. She had not thought that he had been paying such close attention to her. Or, at least, she had not thought he had been doing so to learn something about her. She had thought he was looking for things to criticize. How wrong had she been about him?

Those nerves were once again fluttering, though this time, they were not whispering that she was not good enough for Mr. Darcy. Rather, they were pushing forward the thought that Mary might be right and there was magic at Christmas time, and that, perhaps, just perhaps, there could be a chance that Mr. Darcy might admire her.

No, she scolded herself, that was foolish. He was just being a good host. Surely, it was nothing more. She cast a sidelong glance at him as he reclaimed his seat and indulged in his tea. It was nothing more. It could not be. She would not allow herself to hope. She looked in his direction once more. No matter how much she might wish to do just that.

Chapter 7

Two days later, Darcy looked up from the menu he was reviewing. It was the final bit of business to which he needed to attend this morning. "Can I help you with something?"

"May I come in?" Georgiana asked from the doorway to his study.

"Of course. And then you can look at this and tell me if you think Lady Matlock will think I am nigh onto entering the poorhouse for having a table so poorly turned out or not."

Georgiana giggled and took the paper he held out to her. "You could have twice this much, and she would still worry."

"I see no need to have even that much." He motioned to the page she held. "However, I know we must have a few extras for *my lady*." It was not as if he and Georgiana did without, nor was he miserly about the food he requested for his meals. They were substantial and fitting for his rank. However, Darcy did not approve of excess in most areas of his life, including at his table. His aunt, however, was less disapproving of extravagance.

"Did you not already approve the menu?"

"I did, but Mrs. Latham wished for one final approval." His housekeeper had thought a second meat pie would be a good addition, as would be a glaze for the carrots.

"I think that this appears to be adequate, though I might suggest adding mulled wine to the dessert course."

"Ah, yes, one of Aunt Eleanor's favourite things about the winter months."

Georgiana handed the paper back to him, and he hastily made the additional note before going to the door and asking a footman to see that it was delivered to Mrs. Latham.

"Will it not be nice when you can hand that duty to a wife?"

Darcy turned slowly from the door to face his sister, who happened to be giving her ribbon a close examination. "I am certain I do not need to practice my responses to such questions before our aunt's arrival tonight."

"I was asking for my own curiosity." She peeked up at him.

"Then allow me to satisfy your curiosity by saying I am certain *in a few years* when I am ready to take a wife, it will be a relief to pass to her all the duties that fall within her domain." He stood in front of his desk and leaned against it. "Was there any other reason why you came to visit me?"

Her ribbon was once again of great interest to her. "No."

"Are you certain?" He was not certain.

She opened her mouth but then closed it and shook her head. "There is nothing."

There was not *nothing*. He knew that look. There was something on her mind, but she was not quite ready to share it yet. He could press her to reveal whatever it was. However, he knew that pressing her never worked very well, and since she had just brought up the idea of his marrying, he feared it might be something to do with that. And that was a topic he really had no desire to canvas with his sister – or anyone, for that matter.

"We are calling at the Gardiners' today, are we not?"

He eyed her warily. She knew very well what was planned for this afternoon. "We are taking the Miss Bennets for a drive in Hyde Park because Miss Mary has never been there, and Miss Elizabeth has not been there in a year's time."

Apparently, Mrs. Gardiner made a point of visiting Hyde Park with her nieces when they were in town for "one could not buy a hat if one did not go into a hat shop," which was, of course, a rather clever reference to a lady finding a gentleman at whom to set her cap. Since this was Miss Mary's first time staying with the Gardiners, she had not yet had the opportunity to go to the park.

"Oh, how silly of me to forget." Georgina rose and took his proffered arm.

He doubted very much that she had forgotten. The pink tinge to her cheek and the way her eyes did not meet his were all the proof he needed that he was correct.

"It is too bad that we did not invite the Miss Bennets to dinner so that Aunt and Uncle could meet my new friend."

"Yes, that is too bad." And very purposefully

done, for inviting the Miss Bennets meant inviting not only Miss Mary but also Miss Elizabeth, and ever since Miss Elizabeth had entered his house two days ago after their shopping excursion, Darcy had found that the idea of her becoming Mrs. Darcy had taken deeper root in his mind.

Be that as it may, he was not yet ready to take a wife. Georgiana had a come-out for which to prepare, and he needed to be attentive to all the young gentlemen who came to call or asked for a dance so that he could divine which were worthy and which were fortune hunters. He could not afford to be distracted from such an important task, not even by the pleasant prospect of Miss Elizabeth as his wife. He had very nearly been the source of a miserable future for his sister once already. He would neither fail her nor his mother and father again.

A Darcy did not forget his duty when faced with the prospect of a merry time. He stood his course without wavering – no matter what sacrifice was required. He had heard that very lecture from his father on numerous occasions, beginning when he and Wickham were young.

Wickham, whose father was Pemberley's steward, was often allowed to leave his duties, which had caused some restlessness in Darcy to be off and having fun. However, his father would not hear of it nor would he entertain reasons why he should hear of it. It did not matter to Darcy's father that Wickham was his godson. He was not a Darcy by birth, and no true Darcy was going to regard his duty as something which could be put off.

Of course, the duty to marry and produce an heir was one duty that Darcy was going to put off, but only because his duty to his sister had to come first. He was certain even his father would approve of such a thing.

"I would like our relations to meet my friend."

Darcy nodded. "And perhaps one day they will. However, it will not be today."

They began the ascent of the stairs. "Will you play for me while I read until it is time to go to Gracechurch Street?"

"I would be happy to, but will we not have callers?"

"I have asked that the knocker be removed and all who knock without it to be turned away."

And Beggs would see that no one was admitted, save for the few who were to be admitted no matter if Darcy were home to callers or not, such as Bingley, without his sisters, and his cousin, Colonel Fitzwilliam. Therefore, without fear of any unpleasant interruption, Darcy settled into a chair in the music room with a book to page through while listening to his sister play and attempting not to think about Miss Elizabeth.

~*~*~

Not chuckling while Miss Mary gripped her sister's hand and whispered an excited, "This is it? This is Hyde Park?" was no easy task for Darcy. He was certain he had never met anyone so keenly excited to drive in the park as Miss Mary.

"It is not magical," Miss Elizabeth whispered in reply to her sister. "It is just a park."

Mary's head shook emphatically. "It is not just a park. It is *Hyde Park* where everyone who is anyone is seen."

"There are people from all walks of life here," Miss Elizabeth assured her.

"But not in carriages such as this." Miss Mary sat a little straighter and affected an air of elated nonchalance.

It was most decidedly an elated look, for a lady simply could not look traditionally blasé when her eyes were sparkling, as Miss Mary's were, and when she was biting the corner of her lower lip to keep from smiling broadly, as Miss Mary was. Darcy was certain he was going to enjoy this drive through the park more than he ever had simply because of Miss Mary.

What a thought! To think that the most austere of the Bennet ladies was the lady to bring him such amusement. Of course, the fact that the most animated sister was sitting next to the most enchanting one who was just across from Darcy also helped add to Darcy's enjoyment of the drive.

"That is what is called Rotten Row." Darcy indicated a bridal lane, well-populated by riders, on their left as they entered the park. "And just ahead of us is the Serpentine."

"Oh, it is beautiful," Miss Mary murmured. "Just beautiful. We should walk here," she said, turning to her sister.

"Maybe on another visit," Miss Elizabeth said. "One day when Aunt Gardiner and the children can join us, we will walk here."

"One winter when it got very cold, Fitzwilliam took me skating here," Georgiana said.

"Oh, I think I would like to try skating," Miss Mary cried

"You never have?" Georgiana asked in surprise.

Miss Mary shook her head. "It seemed frivolous." Her eyes grew wide, and she pressed her lips together as if she had misspoken.

"That is what she told our younger sisters when they mentioned skating on a pond," Elizabeth inserted with a reassuring smile for Miss Mary.

How interesting. There seemed to be some secret the two Bennet ladies were keeping.

"I do not truly think it is frivolous," Miss Mary said before turning her eyes back to the park around them. "I think I would rather like skating on the Serpentine."

For twenty minutes, they made their way slowly through the gardens with Miss Mary crying her delight about many things – the turn of a path, the evenness of a stand of trees, the hat of some lady walking on the arm of a soldier, the view of Rotten Row across the Serpentine and glimpsed through the trees, and on and on.

Darcy was quite enjoying himself as he sat and listened to the chatter of the three ladies whom he escorted and who did not once attempt to draw him into their conversation. They did not exclude him either. They were more than delighted when he added a few words now and then. However, he was not the reason for their discussion. He was merely a bystander. It was a lovely change from travelling anywhere with Bingley and his sisters. Miss Bingley and Mrs. Hurst seemed to be always desperate for his input and his approval.

"Darcy!"

"Who is that?" Miss Mary whispered as Darcy turned to see who had hailed him and to signal his driver to stop.

"Bingley said you were in town, but you have not been to our club."

"I have been passing my time with my sister and her friends. You do remember my sister, Georgiana, do you not?"

"I dare say no one could forget such a lovely young lady."

"Hodgkiss," Darcy warned his friend, "she is not out."

"Yes, yes. I know, but that does not mean I must forget her or her beauty."

"I think it does to my brother," Georgiana said with a smile, and – was that a flutter of lashes?

Darcy scowled.

Hodgkiss laughed. "Yes, I dare say it does.

Despite your brother's surly attitude, it is good to see you in such good health, Miss Darcy. Is it not, Pointon?"

"Indeed, it is good to see both you and your brother," Pointon agreed before adding, "and your friends." After giving a nod of his head to Miss Mary and Miss Elizabeth, he turned his attention back to Darcy expectantly.

"Mr. Pointon, Mr. Hodgkiss, this is my sister's friend, Miss Mary Bennet, and her sister, Miss Elizabeth Bennet. Miss Mary, Miss Elizabeth, these gentlemen are friends of myself and Bingley, Mr. Hodgkiss and Mr. Pointon."

"Bennet you say?" Mr. Hodgkiss asked. "Is that not the name Mr. Bingley mentioned?"

"Most likely," Miss Mary answered.

"You know Mr. Bingley?" Mr. Pointon moved his horse closer to Darcy's carriage on the side where Mary sat.

"Netherfield neighbors my father's estate," Mary said before lowering her voice, "and Mr. Bingley did call on our sister Jane while he was in Hertfordshire."

"So, it is the same Bennets," Mr. Hodgkiss said

with a smile. "What brings you ladies to town? The season?"

"No, not yet," Mary answered.

Darcy blinked when Miss Mary ducked her head and peeked up at Mr. Pointon. Had she been taking lessons from her younger sisters? Miss Lydia and Miss Kitty were the only Bennets he had ever seen use such a ploy. Between that and his sister's fluttering of lashes he had witnessed just moments ago, he was reconsidering the friendship between the two.

"But you will be in town for the season?" Mr. Pointon asked.

He seemed eager for a positive reply. Did he find Miss Mary pretty? Darcy supposed she did bear a marked resemblance to Miss Elizabeth, so it was indeed possible.

Miss Mary sighed. "Only for a portion and not as you might expect."

"She means to say we are visiting our aunt and uncle at present and expect to do so again after Christmas." Miss Elizabeth took her sister's hand firmly. "Our aunt and uncle do not attend the soirees of the beau monde."

Excellent! He was not the only one who was

uncomfortable with the flirting. Perhaps, since Miss Elizabeth seemed to have her sister well-in-hand, Georgiana could continue her friendship with Miss Mary.

"Ah," Mr. Hodgkiss said as if everything was perfectly clear to him. "Is your uncle Mr. Gardiner of Gracechurch Street?"

"How do you know that?" Darcy inserted before Miss Elizabeth could reply.

"Bingley," Pointon answered.

"We mean no one any harm, Darcy," Hodgkiss said with a laugh. "However, we might wish to call on two such lovely young ladies as Miss Mary and Miss Elizabeth."

Two young ladies? Darcy's eyes shifted from Hodgkiss to Miss Elizabeth and back. "That will, of course, be up to the young ladies and their uncle."

"I will tell my uncle we would be delighted to receive your call," Miss Mary said nearly before Darcy was done speaking.

"And I will ask Bingley for an introduction to your uncle," Pointon assured her.

"Bingley is returning to Netherfield soon." Darcy wished to rub his chest to soothe his heart, for the thought of any gentleman calling on Miss Elizabeth caused it to ache.

"Not before we get an introduction," Hodgkiss said with a flick of his eyebrows.

What was that supposed to mean? Was Hodgkiss issuing some sort of challenge?

"We will not keep you any longer, Darcy." Hodgkiss gave a nod of his head to Miss Mary and Miss Elizabeth before turning to Georgiana. "It was delightful to see you, Miss Darcy. My day is now brighter."

Georgiana giggled and waved as the man and his friend rode away.

"Mr. Pointon is very handsome," Miss Mary whispered to Georgiana.

"They both are," Georgiana agreed. "Do you not think so?" she asked Elizabeth.

Elizabeth blushed and darted a look in Darcy's direction before giving the slightest nod of her head and causing Darcy to wish to do both of his friends harm.

Chapter 8

As the handsome Mr. Pointon and Mr. Hodgkiss rode away, Elizabeth turned her eyes away from her sister and out to the people and scenery to be found in the gardens. How stupid she had been to hope that Mr. Darcy's remembering the way she took her tea and what sweet she preferred had meant that he might be attracted to her. She should have listened to herself. He was just being a good host, and she was just his sister's friend.

It had been nice, however, to hear herself called a lovely lady by Mr. Darcy's friends. At least, she was not wanting in their eyes. Why must it bother her so much that she was wanting in Mr. Darcy's eyes?

"Do you have a favourite portion of the gardens, Miss Elizabeth?" Mr. Darcy's questions broke into Elizabeth's contemplation.

"I am certain I could not choose just one portion. Every part of it provides such interesting aspects to admire while walking the many paths. Just as you think you have seen the loveliest part; a new vista captures your fancy. Do you have a favourite spot in the park?"

"I think you have said it well," Darcy answered, "though I will admit to enjoying a ride along Rotten Row nearly as much as I do a ramble along the paths. Indeed, I might enjoy riding better." His lips lifted in one of his beautiful smiles.

Oh, why could she not be pretty like Jane?

"Would you care to take a short walk?" he asked. "We have been in the carriage for some time already, and it will be a while before we get back to Gracechurch Street."

"I would not wish to be a bother."

His brow furrowed. "There would be nothing bothersome about it."

"Please, Elizabeth," Mary implored. "I would so like to take a walk on any of the paths – it would not matter which one – just to say I have done it."

"As would I – not that I have not walked on them before," Miss Darcy added.

Elizabeth sighed inwardly. It would mean having to walk with Mr. Darcy, which would be a mixture of discomfort and pleasure. She darted a look at the gentleman as she pretended to look at their surroundings. She could do it. It did not matter, she told herself if he admired her or only thought of her as the sister of his sister's friend, as he had introduced her to Mr. Pointon and Mr. Hodgkiss. She could walk by his side and not feel out of place if she determined to. Indeed, walking with Mr. Darcy might be just the thing for discovering if Mr. Pointon, who appeared to have a fondness for Mary, was a worthy gentleman or not.

Yes, indeed, she could do this for Mary, as well as herself. She might not be the sort of beauty to inspire admiration in Mr. Darcy, but she was not deficient. She had many admirable traits – one of which was being a good sister when Mary needed her to be.

"Will it make you late in returning home?" she asked Mr. Darcy. She knew, from what Miss Darcy had said, that they were expecting their aunt and uncle to join them for dinner.

"Not at all. My uncle never eats early unless he is expected to attend some function."

"Very well. Then, I suppose it would be a fine thing to take a walk."

Mary squealed softly, startling Elizabeth. This new, more exuberant Mary was not easy to adjust to.

"A ride in the park, a walk in the park, and meeting two handsome gentlemen – all in one afternoon! Lydia will be beside herself with jealousy when she hears of it, will she not?" Mary said in a whisper to Elizabeth while Mr. Darcy was requesting that their driver stop to let them out.

"I do not think that making our sister jealous is a proper reason to be pleased about any of those things," Elizabeth replied, keeping her voice just as soft. Surely, there must be something in one of those sermons Mary had read that should remind her that jealousy was not a good thing. If they were not in company, Elizabeth would have reminded Mary of those sermons and asked if any of them had mentioned jealousy in a favourable light or as something to seek. However, Mary's pretense of preferring sermons to any other sort of reading was not something that Elizabeth wished to discuss with Mr. Darcy and his sister.

"I suppose not," Mary acquiesced. "However, it is pleasant to have tried a new experience before Lydia can tell me about it."

"I can approve of that."

Wishing to have tried something before another was not so very bad a thing, was it? Did it not only stray into the unfavourable when a lady sought it at all costs or simply to hold it over another? Did it not come down to a lady's motivation? Was it not of great importance to determine why a lady might want what she wanted?

Elizabeth placed her hand in Mr. Darcy's as he helped her down from his barouche.

For instance, why did she wish so greatly for Mr. Darcy to approve of her? Was it simply because he had injured her pride? She could not believe that such was her reason. As a matter of fact, when her pride had first been injured, she had, in anger, wished for him to think even less of her and then, for something to happen to prove him wrong in a humiliating fashion. That flash of anger had only lasted for a short time before being replaced by a dull, sad ache and a longing for... something. She was not entirely certain what that longing was, though she had her suspicions that it was for him to love her as she...

Her brow furrowed. No, that could not be it?

Could it? Did she love Mr. Darcy – not just admire him, but love him?

"Miss Elizabeth? Is everything well?" Mr. Darcy offered her his arm.

Elizabeth gave herself a mental shake. "Of course, all is well. I was just caught in thought."

"I would say I hope they were happy thoughts, but I must say from your expression, it appeared they were not."

"It was simply a novel thought which surprised me, nothing more." Her cheeks felt a great deal warmer than walking in a park on a cool December day should make them feel. "It is something I will have to ponder later." Much later. When she was no longer walking at his side or in company with her relations. The best thing would be to tuck all thoughts about Mr. Darcy and love away until she was curled up under her covers and the moon was standing sentry over one and all.

"We can walk in silence if you wish to continue your contemplation, or I would be happy to listen if it would help."

"No." That would not help. "Thank you for your kind offer. However, I think it is best saved for later because, at present, I would like to know more about your friends."

The smile he wore faded, and it was three silent strides down the path before he spoke. "What do you wish to know?"

There was a coolness to his tone which caused Elizabeth to pause before gathering her spirit and pressing on. She had a sister to protect and whether Mr. Darcy wished to be surly or not would not stop her from doing so.

"My sister has never had a suitor, and I would like to know that your friends are the sort of gentlemen she should be allowed to entertain. I would not want for her to be taken in by a handsome face and pretty words." Elizabeth smiled as Mary dipped her head close to Georgiana's as they spoke. "She has never even had a friend before," she added softly.

"Truly?"

Elizabeth nodded. "I know she is not all that much younger than me, and I, myself, do not have a great amount of experience with gentlemen callers. However, she is perhaps less prepared for such things since she has not even had a female confidant." Elizabeth blew out a breath. "I thought she was happy on her own." She lifted a shoulder and let it fall as the guilt of having not discovered enough about her younger sister settled over her. "I should have asked her, but... she seemed happy."

"You have not had many callers?"

"No, but that is not the point."

"My apologies. I just find that shocking."

He did?

"I am not sure I understand how that can be shocking since Meryton is not overrun by eligible gentlemen. If you will remember, I was left sitting at the assembly. And, added to that, my sisters are Jane and Lydia. It is hard to compare to either Jane's beauty or Lydia's liveliness." Her cheeks were absolutely burning now. She had never in her life ever admitted such a thing to a gentleman.

"Ah, I see." He looked as if he wished to say more, but as he did not, they once again walked on a few strides in silence.

"Have you known Mr. Hodgkiss and Mr. Pointon for a long time?" Elizabeth asked, bringing the conversation back to what she needed to know.

He nodded. "I have known them for about ten years – since our days at Cambridge."

"And have you been good friends for that whole time?"

"No, but nearly so. Our friendship began a few weeks into our first term."

"Then, you know them well."

"I do."

"And knowing them as you do, would you allow either Mr. Hodgkiss or Mr. Pointon to call on your sister if she were out?"

His head tipped to one side and then the other. "That is a hard thing to answer."

"I do not see how it can be. You are friends with them, and, therefore, you know if they are of sound character, do you not?"

His head bobbed up and down slowly. "Neither Mr. Hodgkiss nor Mr. Pointon is in need of a wealthy wife, nor is either given to the dissipated proclivities of some men of money. However, I struggle to think anyone can truly be worthy of Georgiana." He looked at her. "And how, if I struggle to determine the worthiness of a gentleman for my sister, can I advise you for your sister?"

That made sense, she supposed, and his obvious care for Miss Darcy touched her heart. He was far from the cold man who despised all he saw, as she had first considered him to be a couple of months ago.

"You wish for her happiness, do you not?" she pressed.

"More than anything."

The near agony in his voice when he replied moved her so greatly that it took a moment before she could proceed. Miss Darcy was a fortunate lady to have a brother who loved her so deeply.

"What if your sister loved Mr. Hodgkiss or Mr. Pointon, and whichever gentleman happened to be the happy recipient of such affection returned her love with a fervour that equalled or surpassed yours for her?"

Mr. Darcy stopped walking and stood as if stunned into immobility. "Do you think," he said after a moment of standing silently rooted to the path, "Do you she could love Hodgkiss?"

He turned towards Elizabeth. "Do you think he loves her? I know he likes to flirt with her, but he tends to be charming to everyone. So I have thought nothing of it, other than to consider it an annoyance. Have I missed something?"

Elizabeth giggled at the look of horror he wore. "I do not know, sir. We are just imagining at the moment. I dare say you will not know the gentleman's true feelings on that matter until your sister is out, for he did not strike me as the sort to proceed where it was not proper." Though he did seem the sort to push up against the boundaries, which had been the greatest source of Elizabeth's worry.

"No, no, I suppose you are correct. Hodgkiss is amiable and likes to provoke me, but he is most often proper and most especially so when it comes to young ladies."

Mr. Darcy visibly relaxed before her eyes as he spoke, and his admission that his friend did things to provoke him but was proper calmed Elizabeth's concern about Mr. Hodgkiss.

"Allow me to rephrase my question in a fashion that will not be so disconcerting." She placed her hand back on his proffered arm. "If Mary were to love Mr. Pointon, and he were to love her, should I fear for her happiness?"

Mr. Darcy smiled. "I know you love your sister dearly, but I must admit it is easier to contemplate her loving and being loved than it is my own."

She could not help but laugh lightly at his

admission. "And is it possible then for you to answer for my sister?"

He covered her hand with his free one. "I think it would be a very good match."

"Thank you, Mr. Darcy. You have put this sister's heart at ease."

Chapter 9

"Georgiana was telling me, while we were waiting for dinner to begin, that she wishes to spend Christmas at Netherfield." Darcy's cousin, Colonel Richard Fitzwilliam poured himself a second glass of port before reclining in his chair, which was turned sideways so that he could prop his right arm on the table and so that he was facing Darcy.

"Did she?" Darcy shook his head. "I do not know why she even mentioned it to you. We are not going Netherfield."

Richard shrugged. "She told me you said that as well."

Darcy leaned forward. "Is she playing us against each other again?"

She had done so when she wanted to go to Ramsgate. Richard had been certain a few months near the sea would be good for her constitution.

Darcy had been less sure that the idea was a good one until Richard, with the help of his mother, had convinced Darcy that lots of young ladies travelled to the seaside with companions to no ill effect. It was just how it was done.

Even now, more than six months since that fateful choice had been made, Darcy felt the guilt of being persuaded against his first inclination.

"She might try, but I will not be bamboozled twice." Richard took a large drink from his glass. "I assume you have a reason."

"When does he not?" Lord Matlock said with a chuckle.

"True," Richard agreed.

"Wickham is there," Darcy inserted before he and his penchant for contemplation of all eventualities became fodder for discussion.

Richard's head turned slowly back towards Darcy. "Did I hear you correctly?"

Darcy nodded. "He has joined the militia who are stationed in Hertfordshire."

Richard's eyebrows rose. "Wickham is in the militia?"

Again, Darcy nodded.

"With any luck, they will teach him the discipline he has so far lacked," Lord Matlock muttered.

"I should like to be the colonel of his unit," Richard growled. "How did you come upon this information? Was he there before you left Hertfordshire?"

"He was. He took me quite by surprise. My welcome was not extended." Darcy recalled the anger that burned within him just at the sight of his former friend. "He blanched to see me."

"Excellent," Richard said. "Perhaps your parting words to him found their mark. If they have not, my pistol will."

"I cannot condone such activity," Lord Matlock cautioned. "And my disapproval is nothing to what your mother's would be." He shook his head when Richard opened his mouth to speak. "It does not matter how hideously he has comported himself. A law is a law."

"It is a foolish one. Men ought to be allowed to settle matters of honor on the field."

"You will have to contain such meeting to proper fisticuff matches."

"Father, he did not just toy with Georgiana's

heart by happenstance. He planned the whole scheme well before it ever took place."

"I know what he did. However, allow me to quote my wife. 'The blackguard is not worth your life.'" Lord Matlock raised one eyebrow and gave a nod of his head as if such a quote was the very law on which everything was founded before he took a drink of his own port.

"She is right you know," Darcy agreed. "He is not worth your life, and before you say it, you and I both know your mother was not speaking of you missing your mark. We all know you would not."

"I still think matters of honor should be decided as they used to be."

Lord Matlock shook his head. "How many of those dawn meetings of years gone by could have been avoided and lives saved if all the facts had been discovered before the meeting happened? The ladies are not the only ones who can fly into the rafters over nonsense. Indeed, having been in parliament these many years, I can assure you that some men are more prone to it than their wives or daughters ever would be."

"Be that as it may," Darcy interrupted before Richard and his father began an argument in earnest, "that does not explain why Georgiana is appealing to Richard to go to Netherfield."

Richard finished the port that remained in his glass. "She was not appealing to me. She was merely telling me about her new friend – Miss Mary Bennet, was it not?"

"Yes, that was the name," Lord Matlock agreed. "She speaks very highly of this young lady and her sister." He stood. "And I dare say she is filling her aunt's ears with tales of Miss Mary now." He chuckled. "I do not think I have ever seen her so taken with a friend as she is Miss Mary." He clapped Darcy on the shoulder. "I assume this young lady poses a good friendship for Georgiana?"

"I believe she is."

"And why is that?" Lord Matlock asked.

"She seems mostly sensible." How did he describe the Miss Mary he had met in town?

"Mostly?"

"Yes."

"Which means she is partially nonsensical?" Richard asked.

Darcy released a great heaving sigh and blocked

the dining room door. "I met Miss Mary in Hertfordshire."

"As Georgie said," Richard inserted.

"In Hertfordshire, she wore the plainest dresses I have ever seen on a lady who was not a confirmed old spinster. Her hair was always pulled tightly back in a severe style, and her expression was always on the edge of reproof." He shook his head. "She quoted scripture at the oddest times."

"Such as?" Lord Matlock prompted.

"I heard her quoting some passage to her younger sisters at an assembly." The fact that those younger sisters were likely in need of a sermon was neither here nor there at the moment, for Darcy did not desire to broach that subject with either his cousin or his uncle.

"She sounds...peculiar," Lord Matlock's said.

She was that.

"You said *in Hertfordshire*," Richard said. "Does that mean she is not the same in town?"

Darcy nodded. "She has been fashionably dressed every time I have seen her, and I have yet to hear her quote anything – scripture or otherwise. She seems delighted to be Georgiana's friend, and they get on very well. She is not silly like some young ladies can be, but she is not above flirting."

"Has she flirted with you?" Richard asked in surprise.

Darcy laughed. "No. She thinks nothing of me beyond the fact that I am Georgiana's brother."

Well, that might not be entirely true, for it did seem that Miss Mary was eager to push her sister in his direction. However, that could be just what he was perceiving and not what was actually transpiring so it was best left unsaid.

"Then with whom has she been flirting?" Richard asked.

"Pointon."

"He is a handsome fellow," Lord Matlock said. "And so is his bank account. I can see how a young lady might find him worthy of a flirtation." He looked from Darcy to Richard and back. "What? Am I the only one who listens to Lady Matlock when she talks about who may or may not be a possible match for Georgiana?"

"Apparently so," Richard answered.

"You really should listen to her more often. You would not believe the things I have learned by doing so."

"Has she mentioned Hodgkiss?" Darcy asked.

Lord Matlock nodded. "Charming young chap. Fine looking and well-funded."

"Has she spoken to Georgiana about these things?"

"To whom else would she speak?" Lord Matlock asked in surprise. "She surely was not speaking to me or any of her friends. She would not share such vital information with a potential rival, you see. Why do you ask?"

"I saw Georgiana flutter her lashes at the fellow today when we met him in the park. He was, of course, being his usual, annoyingly charming self."

Lord Matlock chuckled. "And you are surprised by this?"

"You are not?"

His uncle smiled. "No, for I listen to my wife. Now, if you are through telling us about Miss Mary, who sounds like a young lady coming to town for the first time and trying to present herself in a fashion that would attract a young gentleman – which I assure you is perfectly normal – may we proceed to the drawing room?"

"You do not think it is wrong for me to allow a friendship between Miss Mary and Georgie?"

"Not at all. However, I am certain we would like to meet her." He brushed past Darcy. "Do you suppose that her relations would allow her to go to the theater with us?" He stopped in the middle of the hallway. "It would be best if they met us before we extended the invitation." He nodded. "Yes, that is what we will do." Once again, he began walking to the drawing room. "You will have to give me the street and number at which they live."

"I believe Georgiana said they live in Gracechurch Street," Richard said.

Lord Matlock paused at the door to the drawing room which a footman was holding open. "I thought you said your friend was a gentleman's daughter, Georgiana," he called across the drawing room.

"He has been spending far too much time with Mother," Richard whispered with a chuckle. "He will soon be donning a cap, telling tales and having tea with his political cronies' wives."

Darcy joined Richard in a chuckle. His uncle had always been keenly interested in knowing everything that was going on around him, and he likely had several good tales he could tell. However, his lips were not loose, except when he needed them to be. The man was shrewd.

"She is," Georgiana replied.

"Then, why is she staying in Gracechurch Street?"

"Because, my dear, that is where her aunt and uncle live," Lady Matlock answered. "Just because a lady's uncle is not a gentleman does not preclude that her father is also not a gentleman."

Lord Matlock stood before his chair for a moment. "You are correct, my love," he said as he took a seat. "But how did this come to be?"

"I do not know," Lady Matlock said. "Do you, Darcy?"

"Mr. Bennet married the daughter of Meryton's solicitor, and Mr. Gardiner, with whom the Miss Bennets are staying, is Mrs. Bennet's brother."

"Why then is this Gardiner fellow not a solicitor? Is his father still living?" Lord Matlock asked.

"No, his father is not living. His brother-in-law Philips took over the practice."

"The son-in-law taking the business instead of the son? How unusual. Do you know why that is?"

Darcy shook his head in reply to his uncle's question. "I am sorry. I do not."

"You have not asked him?" Lady Matlock asked.

"No. I have not."

"I suppose it might be a bit forward since you have just met them, have you not?"

"Yes, not more than a week ago."

"And how do you find them?" Lady Matlock asked. "Georgiana assures me they are very refined."

"Oh, they are," Georgiana inserted. "Mr. and Mrs. Gardiner both have proper diction and appear to be well-educated. And do you know what Mrs. Gardiner says to her son when he is less than polite?" Her eyes were sparkling with amusement when she peeked at her brother.

"I am certain I could not even guess," Lady Matlock said.

"When we were at their home, we were going to play a game with her two oldest children. The two youngest were in the nursery."

"She had four children?"

Georgiana nodded. "But I have only met two of them, and they are delightful. But as I was saying, Martin – he is the oldest – told us very directly to sit on the floor in a circle. He said it almost like that, too. Well, his mother looked at him with a very severe look and said, 'try again.'"

"As any good mother would," Lady Matlock said with a smile. "I think I would like Mrs. Gardiner."

"I am certain you would," Darcy agreed. "She is as refined as Georgiana says."

"Georgiana said she came to Darcy House and had tea with her nieces after you went shopping."

"She did."

"I hear you also knew exactly how Miss Elizabeth likes her tea."

"Oh, ho!" Richard cried.

"I was less than polite upon our first meeting in Meryton –"

"Yes, so I have heard," Lady Matlock murmured with a tip of her head towards Georgiana when Darcy looked at her in question.

"Miss Mary told me," Georgiana said.

"Well, then, you will understand why I thought it best to *try again* to make a more favourable impression."

Lady Matlock's lips twitched. "I dare say Catherine will be less than pleased to hear her daughter has been thrown over for the niece of a tradesman." She fluttered her lashes at Darcy.

Richard guffawed while Darcy closed his eyes and shook his head.

"I am not throwing Anne over for anyone because we are not betrothed and because I am not looking for a wife."

"I do not know why you are not," Lady Matlock began. "You are not getting any younger. Pemberley needs a mistress and an heir."

"And I assure you that before I am completely old and decrepit, I will do my duty. However, I am not doing it now."

"Oh, but the fun it would be to torment Catherine. Could you not, at least, consider it?"

There was no love lost between his aunts, Lady Matlock and Lady Catherine de Bourgh. Each thought they knew what was best for Darcy, and each laid claim to him. Lady Catherine staked her claim based on his supposed long-standing betrothal to her daughter, Anne, while Lady Matlock claimed Darcy as a third son, which she pointed out was a greater claim than some imaginary childhood marriage agreement.

"Is there something lacking in Miss Mary's sister?" Lord Matlock asked.

"Not at all," Georgiana answered. "She is lovely. Simply lovely."

"Darcy?" His uncle turned to him.

"Georgiana is not given to lying," he replied, although, presently, he wished she were less eager to share everything she knew about the Bennets. "However, I am not of a mind to take any wife at this time, so it is foolish to even consider one."

"Before you begin again with your attempt to persuade Darcy to do what he does not want to do, my love, I wish to tell you that we have decided to call on the Gardiners next week and invite their nieces to the theatre."

"We have?" Lady Matlock asked.

"Indeed, we have, for I think we would both like to meet our niece's and nephew's new friends."

Chapter 10

"Do you like it, Cousin Lizzy?" Nora held her paint-laden brush in the air and peered down at the paper on which she had been painting.

"It is very colourful," Elizabeth said cautiously.

There were bits of red here and green there, but Elizabeth could not discern beyond a shadow of a doubt what each patch of paint represented.

"What is it a painting of?"

She took the brush from Nora's hand and placed it on the tray with the other brushes. Aunt Gardiner was a tremendously good painter, and she insisted upon her children becoming familiar with the activity at an early age, and Uncle Gardiner made certain there was always a good stock of supplies at hand.

"Can you not tell?" Nora asked in surprise.

"What does your mother say about such things?" Mary asked.

"Each person sees paintings in his or her own way," Martin chirped. "You must give it a title if you wish for others to understand what you were trying to show them."

"He is correct," Mary agreed. "While I think your painting looks a great deal like a roaring fire, Lizzy might think it is a bowl made ready for Snap-dragons."

"Ooh, I want to play Snapdragons," Martin said.

"Mama said you could not." Nora looked at her older brother and pursed her lips in a contained smirk.

The two of them had been at odds for most of the morning.

"I can still want to play it," Martin grumbled.

"Indeed, you can," Mary inserted with a plead-ing look to Elizabeth.

"What is the title of your painting, Nora?" Eliza-beth asked.

"I do not know," Nora answered with a shrug of her shoulders.

"Tell me what you see in the painting," Elizabeth

encouraged, "and Mary and I will help you with a title."

"That is Papa's chair where he always reads to us." Nora pointed to a blob of red on the left side of the painting. "That is the carpet where we sit unless it is our turn to sit on Papa's lap." This time she pointed to a patch of green that had been dotted with blue and yellow. "This is the window with snow outside, and this is the warm fire." She indicated each item.

"That sounds very cozy," Elizabeth said.

"And very much like things you love," Mary added.

Nora nodded. "I do. Very much."

"Elizabeth, Mary, we have callers." Aunt Gardiner stood at the door to the dining room where the children had been allowed to set up their art studio.

"Do we?" Mary asked eagerly. "Is it Mr. Pointon?" she whispered.

Mary had come home yesterday from their drive and shared in great detail, at least twice, all she knew about Mr. Pointon, which was more than Elizabeth had known. Apparently, Miss Darcy was more willing to share information about a handsome young gentleman than her older brother was. Uncle Gardiner had assured Mary, upon each recitation, that should Mr. Hodgkiss and Mr. Pointon present themselves to him at his warehouse, he would be certain to grant them his permission to call on Mary and Elizabeth, and so, Mary was eagerly awaiting her first call from a gentleman.

"No, it is not, Mr. Pointon," Aunt Gardiner answered. "It is Miss Darcy, Mr. Darcy, and their cousin, Colonel Fitzwilliam, along with his parents," she closed her eyes and shook her head as if she could not believe what she was about to say, "Lord and Lady Matlock." She placed a hand on her heart and blew out a breath. "The earl and countess of Matlock are in my sitting room... in Gracechurch Street."

"A real lady?" Nora's eyes were wide.

Her mother nodded. "Mr. Darcy's aunt is indeed a real lady."

"May I meet her? Please, Mama?" Nora hopped down from the chair on which she had been kneeling while painting.

"Yes, yes. You may both meet our guests before you return to the nursery." She looked to Elizabeth and Mary. "Can you see the children to the sitting room? I dare not make our guests wait any longer."

"Of course," Elizabeth assured her. "Come, Nora, let me see you. Turn." There were no smudges of paint on Nora's face or in her hair, as sometimes happened. Satisfied that her cousin was presentable, Elizabeth removed the apron Nora was wearing before removing her own.

"Do I have any paint on my face?" she asked Nora, who shook her head.

Elizabeth touched her hair, hoping that it was presentable.

While she had told herself after yesterday's drive that hoping for Mr. Darcy to admire her as more than the friend of his sister was foolish, her heart refused to listen, and if hearts could dance, hers would be doing so now merely because Mr. Darcy was in her aunt's sitting room. There was no hope for it. She was likely going to take a broken heart home to Longbourn when the time came to leave Gracechurch Street.

"You look pretty," Nora said.

Elizabeth smiled. "Pretty enough to meet a real lady?"

Nora nodded and took Elizabeth's hand.

"Are you and Martin ready?" she asked Mary.

"Indeed, we are."

Together, the group of painters sedately made their way to the sitting room, while Elizabeth's heart attempted to run ahead of them.

"I do hope our call is not an imposition," Lady Matlock was saying as Elizabeth entered the room. Lady Matlock wore an elegant dark blue gown that set off her eyes to best advantage. One eyebrow arched as she turned her attention to Elizabeth and surveyed her from head to toe before smiling in a most pleased fashion.

"Not at all, my lady. I indulged the children with a longer than usual painting time this morning. Oh, and here they are."

Elizabeth had never seen Aunt Gardiner look so ill-at-ease.

"My lord, my lady, and Colonel Fitzwilliam, may I present my nieces and my two eldest children?"

"Please," Lord Matlock said. He wore a blue jacket constructed of noticeably fine material that complimented his wife's gown, and while he held himself rather regally, his eyes and smile were kind.

"This is my niece, Miss Elizabeth Bennet," Aunt Gardiner said, "and with her, is my daughter, Nora.

Then, we have my other niece, Miss Mary Bennet, and with her, is my eldest son, Martin. Children, Lizzy, Mary, this is Lord Matlock, Lady Matlock, and Colonel Fitzwilliam. They are Mr. and Miss Darcy's uncle, aunt, and cousin."

"And we are delighted to meet you," Lord Matlock said as they all took their seats. "Miss Darcy has had a great deal to say about her new friend. So much, in fact, that we could not wait to make ourselves known to you, Miss Mary."

Mary ducked her head. "I am honoured, my lord."

The pleased-beyond-measure smile Mary wore delighted Elizabeth. She knew that no one had ever called specifically to make Mary's acquaintance. That the people who chose to do so were an earl and countess only added depth to the honour bestowed on her sister. She glanced at Mr. Darcy who was watching her and smiled. She would have to thank him for bringing his relations to Gracechurch Street and making Mary feel so special.

"Yes, we were quite intrigued," Lady Matlock agreed before she turned to Nora. "Your mother said you were painting."

Nora nodded and squeezed Elizabeth's hand, which she had refused to release, more tightly. "Yes, my lady."

"I like painting," Lady Matlock continued. "What was the subject of your endeavour?"

Nora looked at Elizabeth with wide eyes.

"She wants to know what you were painting," Elizabeth said softly.

"I never named it," Nora whispered.

"Just describe it as you did to Mary and me," Elizabeth encouraged.

"I like painting pictures of fruit," Lady Matlock said as her attention shifted from Elizabeth back to Nora. "They sit very still. I have yet to have one run away on me."

Nora giggled.

"Did you paint fruit?" It was clear that Lady Matlock was just as enamored with Nora as Nora was with her.

Nora shook her head. "I painted a picture from my head."

"Oh! How very impressive," Lady Matlock said. "Does your painting have a name?"

Nora tapped her lip with the finger of her free

hand. "I think," she said and then paused, "I think I will call it 'My Cozy Heart.'"

"Hearth," Martin corrected.

Nora shook her head. "No, heart."

"There was no heart in your picture."

"Martin," Aunt Gardiner scolded, "allow your sister to explain."

Martin pressed his lips together and looked chagrined.

"Why is it called that?" Aunt Gardiner asked Nora.

"Because Cousin Lizzy said it looked cozy, and everything in it is something I love."

"Then it is a very good name," her mother assured her. "Would you not agree, Martin?"

"Yes, ma'am," Martin replied. "It is a good name, Nora. I liked the fire the best."

Lady Matlock's lips twitched with amusement, and her eyes darted to Mr. Darcy, causing Elizabeth to wonder just how often the gentleman had been corrected as Martin often was.

"There was also a chair that her father sits in to read her stories and a window showing the snow falling outside," Elizabeth added.

"And a rug," Nora reminded her. "That is where

I sit when Papa reads unless it is my turn to sit in his lap," she explained to Lady Matlock.

"Excellent. It sounds simply marvelous." Having thoroughly delighted Nora with her response, Lady Matlock turned her attention to Martin. "And Master Gardiner, what did you paint?"

"A bridge and carriages."

"And a road," Nora added.

"Yes, and a road," Martin agreed.

That might have been the first time they had agreed in the past hour.

"That sounds like an excellent subject to paint," Lady Matlock assured him as a maid entered with a tea tray.

"And now, Martin and Nora, I think it is time for you to return to the nursery," Mrs. Gardiner said. "Molly has likely taken your tea up before bringing us ours."

Nora popped off the chair into which she had squeezed herself next to Elizabeth.

"Before you leave," Aunt Gardiner said with a meaningful look and a slight tip of her head toward their guests.

"It was a pleasure to meet you," Martin said before giving a very proper bow.

"Indeed, it was," Nora agreed with a curtsey. "I do hope you will call again."

Amusement sparkled in Lady Matlock's eyes, while her husband smiled broadly.

"We would be delighted to call again," Lord Matlock said. "You are both very well-behaved children."

"Thank you, my lord," Martin replied before turning to his sister and extending his arm. "Nora."

His sister smiled and placed her hand on his arm just as they always practised doing when going in to dinner.

"I liked your bridge," Nora said to her brother as they left the room.

Aside from the tendency the two had to argue with each other, they really were loving siblings.

"They are sweet children," Lady Matlock said to Mrs. Gardiner.

"Thank you, my lady." She rose to pour the tea, and Mary followed to help.

"It looks as if I am just in time," Uncle Gardiner said as he entered the sitting room.

"Mr. Gardiner, I presume," Lord Matlock rose to greet him.

"You would be correct, my lord."

"My wife, Lady Matlock, and my second son, Colonel Fitzwilliam," he said with a sweep of a hand toward his wife and son. "We have just concluded a delightful discussion of art with two of your children."

Uncle Gardiner smiled. "Nora likes to paint nearly as much as my wife does." He settled into a chair close to Lord Matlock.

"Your tea, Lizzy," Mary said.

"Thank you."

"Would you like my seat?" Mr. Darcy asked Mary.

"I would not wish to be an imposition," Mary replied.

"I am positive my sister would rather sit by you than me," he assured her with a smile.

"If that is the case..." She looked at Georgiana who nodded. "Then, yes, I would gladly take your place, Mr. Darcy, just as soon as I gather my tea."

Darcy rose and moved to the chair just to Elizabeth's left.

"That was kind."

"No, it was not."

"I believe it was, sir."

He shook his head. "Georgiana kept poking me.

It was self-preservation." His lips tipped into one of his beautiful smiles.

"Sisters can be a trial." Elizabeth laughed lightly. "Be thankful you only have one."

Darcy chuckled. "I am. Believe me. I am." He took a sip of his tea. "Georgiana is a good sister, though we do, on occasion, argue much like your cousins do."

"We cannot all be so perfect as Jane." Elizabeth hid her smile behind her cup.

"Does Miss Bennet not argue?"

"Rarely. However, that is not to say she does not disagree with anyone. It is just that she sees no need to do more than state her opinion. She saves the defense of her opinion to a well-placed comment such as 'I do believe that is what I said' once her opinion has been proven correct."

Mr. Darcy chuckled. "And what of your other sisters? Do they argue?"

"Yes, though it is Lydia who is the most vehement in attempting to gain her point."

"I can see that," Mr. Darcy said. "She seems very self-assured and exuberant."

"She is." Elizabeth turned her attention back to her tea, glancing to her right as Mr. Darcy's cousin took a seat next to her. He was a handsome enough gentleman, though his pleasant features paled in comparison to Mr. Darcy.

"I hope you do not mind if I join you," he said.

"Not at all," she assured him.

"Do not stop your conversation on my account," he added.

"I believe it was done." What more was there to say on the subject of argumentative siblings?

"I understand you met my cousin when he was in Hertfordshire."

Elizabeth glanced at Mr. Darcy. "I did."

"And did he make a favourable impression?" The colonel's lips tipped up as if he already knew the answer to that question.

"No, I did not." Mr. Darcy's brusque reply surprised Elizabeth. "I was reluctant to dance and critical when pushed to do so." He leveled a hard stare at his cousin.

Elizabeth's eyes shifted from Mr. Darcy to his cousin and back.

"That was not very gentlemanly of you, Darcy."

"No, it was not."

Apparently, the glare Mr. Darcy wore did little to discomfit his cousin since the colonel continued to look amused. Elizabeth had endured a morning of arguing from children. As she sipped her tea, she hoped that she was destined to withstand the same sort of repartee from the gentlemen who flanked her.

"He has been exemplary while in town," Mary inserted.

Elizabeth had not been aware that Mary and Georgiana had been listening, but she was glad for it.

"Indeed, he has," she agreed with alacrity. Hopefully, doing so would put an end to whatever disagreement Mr. Darcy and his cousin were about to have. She often enjoyed a lively debate, but honestly, her ears were tired. Nora had been excessively talkative today.

"I think everyone, no matter their station, is allowed to be out of sorts and disagreeable at times, do you not agree?" Mary asked Colonel Fitzwilliam.

Oh, dear. Mary was not attempting to provoke the colonel, was she?

"That is not to say, of course, that such behaviour is acceptable and should not be remedied,"

Mary continued without giving anyone the opportunity to answer.

Ah, it was to be a lecture and not a discussion. Mary often used this technique when scolding Lydia. Elizabeth's eyes darted to the colonel. Hopefully, he responded with greater dignity and restraint that Lydia ever did to one of Mary's lectures.

"Anyone who has spent any time at all listening to the parson on a Sunday morning would know that he or she would need to repent for their poor behaviour and turn away from it. Is that not right?" Mary asked the colonel again. "And the offended should grant forgiveness – not that doing so removes the consequences of one's actions – there is the stain of sin and all that."

The colonel's jaw had gone slack as Mary continued with her lecture.

Mary's focus sifted from Mr. Darcy's cousin to her sister. "Would you not agree, Elizabeth?"

"Yes?" Elizabeth said in surprise. Was Mary asking her to forgive Mr. Darcy for his harsh words at the assembly? Her brow furrowed.

"I am glad you agree," Mary replied with a satisfied smile. "You see, that is why Aunt Gardiner tells Martin to begin again. It is not that what he has done is erased. We all remember it. However, by turning him from his wrongdoing and towards producing proper behaviour, our aunt draws her son closer to the man she wishes for him to become." She shifted her attention to Mr. Darcy. "I think Mr. Darcy has done a masterful job of beginning again." Her eyes returned to Elizabeth. "Do you not agree, Lizzy?"

Heat raced into Elizabeth's cheeks. Mary was correct. That was the most annoying part of Mary's sermons. She was often right. Elizabeth had to admit that Mr. Darcy had shown himself to be the opposite of how he had presented himself upon their first meeting. She looked from Mary to Mr. Darcy.

"Yes, he has," she admitted.

Mr. Darcy's features relaxed while a stirring softness entered his eyes as his gaze held hers.

"And it would be extremely poor manners on our part to bring what is forgiven as a charge against another after the blunder has been forgiven, especially at Christmas time when we remember the birth of our Savior. However, that is another topic for another time." Mary pressed her lips together as if she had just remembered that she was no longer the sister who gave sermons.

"It is a good reminder," Miss Darcy said.

"Indeed, it is," her brother agreed.

"That was quite the defense of my cousin," Colonel Fitzwilliam said. "You must think very highly of him."

"Perhaps I did not at first, but, having gotten to know him as I have in the past few days and from his sister's accounts, yes, I esteem him greatly."

Mary's reply echoed Elizabeth's own thoughts. She did not just admire Mr. Darcy because he was handsome. She esteemed Mr. Darcy for his character, and not just as one might do the brother of a friend. No, as she saw clearly now, it was more than that. She held him in the highest regard a lady could hold a gentleman. She loved him.

Chapter 11

As Darcy stood with his chin lifted, looking down his nose into the mirror so he could watch his man tie his cravat, he once again allowed his mind to wander back to three days ago when Miss Mary had told him he had succeeded in beginning again and Miss Elizabeth had agreed. Not even honey, eaten straight from the honeycomb, was so sweet as those words of agreement had been.

In the moment, he had forgotten himself and allowed his admiration for Miss Elizabeth to shine in his expression. It had been a mistake, for it had not gone unnoticed. Richard had been unbearable on the ride home, and neither his mother nor his father had discouraged him from his persistent teasing.

Darcy had been contemplating his predicament for three and a half days and three nights. His position was precarious, for he felt as if he was on the precipice of irrevocably losing his heart to Miss Elizabeth, especially if her eyes were to continue to reflect his admiration back to him as she had on that day at the Gardiners.

He blew out a slow breath as his valet moved behind him and ran his hands across Darcy's shoulders, ensuring that all was as it should be.

"You have done an excellent job, as usual, Henry."

The man thanked Darcy with a nod of his head and then, busied himself straightening the dressing room, while Darcy exited his room.

"You look just like Father," Georgiana greeted him as he joined her to go down the stairs.

"And you are very much the image of Mother." There was no denying that his little sister was leaving her childhood behind. She looked every inch the part of a debutante.

"Do you truly think so? She was so beautiful, or, at least, the pictures I have seen of her are."

Darcy nodded. "I do think so. And yes, she was beautiful with a beauty that radiated from deep within her. I see not only her face and figure when

I look at you, Georgiana. I see her spirit shining in your eyes."

"Oh, Fitzwilliam, do not make me cry. A red nose and eyes would not go well with my ensemble."

He covered her hand which lay on his arm as they descended the grand staircase. "I will not say another sentimental thing, for I have an image to retain. I am not Fitzwilliam Darcy, the maudlin master of Pemberley, after all."

Georgiana laughed as he knew she would. "No," she agreed, "you are the good master of Pemberley and the most wonderful brother."

He cast a skeptical glance at her. "You are not going to ask me if you can go to Netherfield again, are you?" There had been small hints about her desire to spend Christmas with Miss Mary nearly every day.

"I will not ask," she assured him. "However, I cannot help it if I mention my hopes and dreams, can I?"

He shook his head and sighed.

"You are a good brother, Fitzwilliam, whether we spend Christmas in town or at Netherfield with our friends. No lady has been given a better brother." She fluttered her lashes at him as her maid helped her into her wrap.

"When you do that, I have no idea if you are being honest or hoping to coerce me," Darcy said as he buttoned his greatcoat.

"Can it not be both?" she teased.

"I would prefer one over the other." He put his hat on and held out his hand to her.

Her spirit was most certainly returning to how it had been before her ordeal at Ramsgate. She had always been a bit of a plotter. She liked patterns, and she had a keen mind to see how things connected. She had always claimed that it was the patterns and connections which made music so fascinating to her. Those same traits had helped her excel at playing chess. Darcy never had to let her win. When she won, it was all thanks to her clever mind and her own efforts.

Wickham had known that about her, and he had played to that part of her temperament – just as he had played to the tender heart he knew she possessed. Was there a blacker blackguard? To Darcy's mind, there was not.

"This feels like practice for my season," his sister said as she settled into their carriage, which would take them, first, to the Gardiners' residence and then, to the theatre where they would meet Lord and Lady Matlock for a play.

"In a way, it is, I suppose," he allowed. "However, tonight, you are not to flirt with any gentlemen, for you are not yet out." Even if she looked as if she were ready to be out, he was not ready for her to be.

"I know." The words were followed by a frustrated huff.

He should likely stop reminding her that she was not out. It was not as if she was going to forget herself or purposefully behave in an improper fashion. While she had made a mistake in trusting Wickham and had allowed herself to be bent to agree to his duplicitous plans, she had not been able to complete the deception. It was not she whom he struggled to trust. It was every gentleman who saw her as a possible wife and his own ability to guide her to a happy future that he doubted.

"May I speak to a gentleman if he is known to me and I to him?"

Darcy sighed. "I suppose I must allow it."

"Though you would rather not."

He nodded as the carriage began to move. He was not eager for her to move from the sister she had always been to the lady she was destined to become. "I will admit to not looking forward to your season with any great amount of excited anticipation."

She smiled and turned her attention to the shadows and figures that could be seen along the lamplit streets.

For several minutes, they rode in silence.

"Fitzwilliam?"

"Yes."

"Why do you fear my season?"

"I did not say I feared it." Fear sounded like something which was far too cowardly to admit.

"Oh, no, you never do," she hurried to assure him. "At least, you do not do so with words, but you grimace when I speak of my season as if the thought of it causes you pain. I know you try to hide your discomfort, but I see it."

He would need to do a better job of concealing his unease. "I do not enjoy the season." It was a true statement, and yet, a niggling of guilt pricked his mind for it was not the sole reason for his discomfort regarding her season. However, he did not wish to discuss the rest.

He saw her head shake from side to side. He was

not going to be fortunate enough to leave his reply at that.

"That is only part of why you dread my season."

Dread was a good word for how he felt about presenting her to a society in which charlatans stood shoulder to shoulder with gentlemen of excellent character and who could not be detected just with a glance. Sometimes, even a thorough appraisal of their person did nothing to reveal the worthy from the unworthy, and it was not just the gentlemen who posed such a puzzle. The same disguise was worn by ladies who pretended to be friends but were just as eager to use a friend to gain an advantage as a rogue was to use a lady for his own pleasure. Both were looking to sate their own desires, and a tender-hearted, trusting miss could be grievously hurt. With such a set of players mixed into the faces of people Georgiana would meet, how could he not dread being her sole defense against such scoundrels? There was no room for error in performing his role as guardian, and if he had not learned it from his father's instruction, he had most certainly gained the knowledge that he was not infallible from the whole debacle at Ramsgate.

"Is it because I was foolish and believed Mr. Wickham?"

Darcy sighed. This was one time he had hoped her ability to make connections would not be so good. "Yes, but not because of you. I should have known –"

"What?" she interrupted. "What should you have known?"

That was a question which, should he answer it as he wished, would only lead to an argument he was unlikely to win, as Georgiana assuredly knew. He knew he could not have known about the duplicity of Georgiana's companion or the treachery Wickham had devised, and if he knew that fact, Darcy had no doubt that his sister would also know it.

"I should not have allowed you to go to Ramsgate. I had refused and then was persuaded."

The carriage fell into silence again for several minutes.

"I should have gone with you." He closed his eyes. How many times had he replayed the incident trying to find ways that it could have been prevented?

"Not every untoward thing can be prevented," she said softly.

"I know."

"Is that why you fear my season?"

He turned his gaze toward the window. "I suppose it is," he admitted softly.

There was a rustling of skirts as Georgiana crossed to sit next to him.

"This," she whispered, "this love you have for me, is why you are such a good brother. I promise you that I will not be so easily duped as I was with Mr. Wickham and that I will seek your counsel, as well as that of Richard and our aunt and uncle. I will do what I can to make your duty lighter."

Her words were filled with the wisdom he might have expected from a lady much older, not his younger sister. She was ready to face her season in more than just appearance. He took her hand and gave it a squeeze. "Thank you."

She placed a kiss on his cheek before resting her head against his shoulder. "A wife could make your duty lighter still," she whispered.

"Georgiana," he scolded. "I do not wish to hear about my need for a wife tonight." He had enough troubling thoughts running in those directions as it was.

"It is just a thought you should consider. I will say no more."

She might not say any more on the topic, but he was certain that neither Richard nor Lady Matlock would be so obliging as to refrain from comment on the fact that he was not yet married.

~*~*~

Much to Darcy's dismay, he was not wrong. His aunt was indeed of a mind to mention marriage several times before the first intermission. However, he had not been the only one to be gathered under her net of suggestions.

"I understand you are to come to town during the season," Lady Matlock said to Miss Mary. "You will have to join us for an evening at the theatre then, just as you are now."

"I would like that very much, my lady."

"And, I could... perhaps... if it were acceptable to your aunt and uncle... maybe... introduce you to a few gentlemen," Lady Matlock added, causing Richard to chuckle, as he rose from his chair and shifted toward the door. He often made a hasty escape during the intermissions so that he could avoid his mother's machinations.

"I would like that very much, my lady," Miss Mary replied.

"Take care, Miss Mary," he said. "She finds games of strategy, such as matchmaking, to be highly diverting."

"That does not scare me, Colonel," Miss Mary replied.

She was as lively tonight as Darcy had ever seen her. The theatre seemed to delight her above anything she had ever experienced. Her excitement upon arriving had been ten times greater than it had been when they entered Hyde Park on their drive. It made him wonder what other entertainments might also prompt such a light-hearted countenance in Miss Mary. The transformation in her from what he had seen of her in Hertfordshire was truly remarkable.

"You are either courageous or unwise," Richard responded from where he stood at the entrance to his father's box.

"I am afraid it is neither, sir," Miss Mary said. "While I have not been the subject of any matchmaking schemes, I can assure you I have witnessed many."

"Have you, indeed?" Richard took a step back toward where Mary was sitting. She had obviously piqued his interest.

"Oh, yes. My mother is spectacularly good at promoting her daughters. Well, other than me and Lizzy, that is."

Richard's curiosity seemed thoroughly aroused, and his quest to escape seemed all but forgotten.

"And why, pray tell, does your mother not promote you?" he asked.

Miss Mary blinked as if the answer to such a question was plainly obvious. "Because I do not wish it."

From the way Richard's brow furrowed, it was not the response he was expecting. Indeed, Darcy had not expected such an answer either. Again, he began to wonder about the Miss Mary who sat next to his sister in front of him.

"One does not avoid a matchmaking mother just because one does not wish to be matched," Richard scoffed.

Miss Mary chuckled. "One does if one goes about it correctly, Colonel."

Richard shook his head as if befuddled. "I am certain there is no way to go about it *correctly*."

"Or he would have found it years ago," Lady Matlock said with a laugh. "I have been attempting to get him or his brother or his cousin," she gave Darcy a pointed look, "to come up to scratch, but I have failed time and time again." She turned her attention to Richard. "Would either you or your sister like to marry my son?" Her lips pursed in amusement.

"I am sorry, but I do not, my lady," Miss Mary said softly.

Richard looked affronted. "And why would you not? Not that I am offering. I am merely curious."

Miss Mary looked around the box. "Must I answer? I am certain you do not wish to know."

If Richard did not wish to know, Darcy did.

"I would not ask if I did not want to know the answer." Richard's words were clipped. Apparently, Miss Mary had thoroughly ruffled the colonel's feathers by contradicting him at every turn.

"It is your profession," Miss Elizabeth said with a small smile for her sister. "However, we do have a younger sister or two who is excessively fond of a scarlet coat."

"How young?" Lady Matlock asked.

"My age, or just about," Georgiana replied.

"Both of them?"

Miss Mary nodded.

"A young wife is not so bad a thing," she said.

Richard held up his hands. "No, Mother, I am not looking for a wife."

"Neither is Darcy, but that does not mean you both do not need one." Her eyes flicked from Darcy to Miss Elizabeth and back, leaving no doubt in Darcy's mind as to whom she was suggesting as a wife for him.

"Why are young men not looking for wives these days?" Lord Matlock interjected. "I have found that having a wife has made my life so much better than it possibly could have been without one."

"Just because Darcy and I are not looking for wives at present," Richard retorted, "does not mean we will not be looking at some point. And when we are, we would like to be able to find them without my mother's scheming."

"I still do not understand the reluctance," Lord Matlock said. "It is youthful ignorance."

"Be that as it may, things are as they are," Richard held his father's gaze for a moment before turning back to Miss Mary. "What is wrong with my profession?"

"Nothing," she said quickly. "Soldiers are needed. Lands and citizens must be defended. It is a noble profession. It is just not one to which I would want to be married, and I do believe I am allowed to have a preference about such things."

"I suppose you are," he replied. "However, I still do not understand why you would refuse a man based on a profession which you call noble."

Miss Mary said no more.

After a moment of holding Miss Mary's unwavering gaze, Richard turned away. "I shall return." He paused once more at the door. "I would still like to know your reason," he said to Miss Mary.

"I am not giving it," Mary assured him.

Displeasure etched his features as he turned away. "Gentlemen," he greeted when he opened the door to find Mr. Pointon, Mr. Hodgkiss, and Bingley about to knock. With a wave of his hand, he motioned for them to enter before he ducked out.

"Darcy," Bingley said by way of greeting once he and his friends had been welcomed by Lord and Lady Matlock, "I saw you and thought I would come to see what you have been about."

"I thought you had returned to Netherfield."

"I did, but I came back to town on business."

"Business? I thought you completed all that needed completing before you left town. What business brings you back?"

A smile spread across his friend's face.

"I am not at liberty to officially say," he whispered rather loudly, "but it seems you were correct about your sister welcoming my return, Miss Elizabeth."

Mary gasped. "Are you and Jane betrothed?" she whispered.

"I am here to see my solicitor about some papers," Bingley replied.

"Finally! A gentleman who is not afraid to marry," Lord Matlock said.

"Who is afraid to marry?" Bingley asked.

"My son and my nephew."

Darcy shook his head. It was the second time

he had been accused of being afraid of something! "No one is afraid to marry, my lord. It is just not the appropriate time." He rose. He had had his fill of sitting.

"Perhaps you should escort your sister and her friends on a short stroll," Lady Matlock said before Darcy could take more than a step away from his chair. "And Mr. Bingley, Mr. Pointon, and Mr. Hodgkiss can accompany you." She shared a speaking look with Georgiana, who blushed.

He would have to ask his sister about that later. For now, he just wanted to be out of this box before either his aunt or his uncle could once again bring up the topic of marriage. He was not yet prepared to take a wife. He had a duty to fulfill to his sister, and a wife would be a distraction.

"It would be my pleasure."

His aunt raised a questioning eyebrow to which he replied with a shrug. What was he supposed to say? *No, I would rather walk by myself to avoid being with Miss Elizabeth because I find myself drawn to her and, without your help, contemplating giving up my duty to fulfill my desire to marry her?* That would not do. Therefore, he would pretend that escorting his sister, who was once again fluttering her lashes at Hodgkiss, would be a joy.

Chapter 12

Mary nudged Elizabeth forward as they both moved away from their seats in the theatre box.

"I am walking with Miss Darcy," she whispered to the back of Elizabeth's head before giving her another poke from behind and toward Mr. Darcy.

Mr. Darcy looked from Mary to his sister.

"They wish to walk together," Elizabeth explained.

His lips flicked up in a tight smile before he offered her his arm. "Then, I suppose it is up to me to accompany you."

"It appears that is our fate." It also appeared as if it were a fate he would rather avoid. "If you prefer, I can insist on walking with my sister."

"No, I would not wish to come between our sisters and their enjoyment of the evening."

"This arrangement might not be all bad." Elizabeth did her best to sound hopeful. "If we allow our sisters to walk ahead of us, we can keep watch over how they interact with Mr. Pointon and Mr. Hodgkiss." That earned her a proper smile from the gentleman whose arm she held.

"I say, Miss Elizabeth," Mr. Bingley said as he joined her and Mr. Darcy in the corridor in front of the door to the Matlock's box, "it seems as if Miss Mary is enjoying her time in town."

"She is thoroughly pleased with the experience." And Elizabeth was delighted to see just how much Mary seemed to be relaxing into the new, livelier version of herself that she longed to be. "I fear no one will recognize her when we return to Longbourn in a fortnight."

"It will be a treat to see," Mr. Bingley agreed with a laugh. "I have mentioned the change in Miss Mary to Miss Bennet but no one else."

"How is Jane?"

"Beautiful as ever."

"Mr. Bingley," Lord Matlock called, "if I could have a word."

"It seems a poor idea to refuse the Earl of Matlock a request," he said with a nod of his head in parting.

Elizabeth had hoped to hear more about her family, but she had to agree that giving precedence to the earl of Matlock was best.

When she turned her attention back to Mr. Darcy, he was looking into the theatre box with a furrow in his brow and appeared to be deep in thought and as if he had forgotten he was supposed to be strolling with her.

"Our sisters may get lost if we remain standing here."

His attention snapped back to her and then fixed on something ahead of him. "I suppose you are correct."

They began walking down the corridor behind Mary and Miss Darcy, who were flanked by Mr. Pointon, on Mary's side, and Mr. Hodgkiss, on Miss Darcy's side. Groups of well-dressed men and women shifted along the hall with them. Some were strolling just as she was with Mr. Darcy, while others were standing about in groups conversing. Elizabeth admired the dresses and hats of the ladies they passed.

"Are you enjoying the play?" Mr. Darcy asked.

"I am, and you?"

He nodded without saying a word, which

seemed an odd response from someone who had just started a conversation.

"Before we part ways tonight," Elizabeth said in an attempt to begin some sort of discussion, "my uncle has made me promise to extend an invitation to you and Miss Darcy to dine with us in Gracechurch Street a week from today."

"I will speak to Georgiana about it."

He fell silent again. There was just something that seemed different about him tonight. It was almost as if he did not want to be where he was.

"My aunt Gardiner wished to know if there are any foods which are traditional in your home around the holidays which she could add to her table."

"That is kind. I am sure Georgiana will be able to tell you about them." He glanced at her and then focused his eyes ahead of them again.

Was he determined to not speak with her?

"I wanted to thank you for introducing your relations to mine. Ever since she met your aunt, Nora has not stopped talking about the real lady who visited her."

"I am glad I could bring your cousin some joy."

"Martin might be happier if you had not, for he

has little patience for listening to the same story over and over." The comment drew a small chuckle from Mr. Darcy.

"My apologies to Master Gardiner."

She waited for several steps to see if he was going to show any interest in taking up his part of the conversation. He did not.

"Would you rather that I return to the box?" she asked, keeping her voice low.

Finally, he turned towards her for longer than the few seconds it took to glance to his side. "Do you wish to?" he asked in surprise.

"I wish to not be a bother to you, Mr. Darcy."

He seemed to hesitate before saying, "You are not."

"I am." She withdrew her hand from his arm.

"You are leaving me?" He still seemed shocked over her decision to not continue with him on his silent walk.

"It seems best."

"I apologize, but I do not know why you would think so. What about your sister?"

"She seems to be in good company. I see no reason to fear for the safety of her person or reputation. You did tell me that Mr. Pointon was a man of good character, and he seemed to be so when he called on us yesterday."

"He called on you?"

She shook her head. "He called on Mary. I cannot tell you how overjoyed she was to receive a call from a gentleman."

"Did he come alone?"

Her brow furrowed. "No, Mr. Hodgkiss was with him."

"Then, Mr. Hodgkiss called on you?"

Mr. Darcy's eyes turned away from her again. She followed the line of his sight. Ah! That was what had him distracted. Mr. Hodgkiss was walking with his sister. She remembered how that particular arrangement had put him ill-at-ease in the park.

"No, he just accompanied his friend. If I were asked to share my thoughts about that gentleman's interest, I would say they do not lie with me but are engaged elsewhere, for he asked about your sister twice while he was at Gracechurch Street."

"Did he?" The words were frigid.

"He asked about her as it related to our having seen your sister. I assure you it was nothing improper. I would venture to say that he knows she is not out, and he respects you far too much to anger you by being too forward. Look at him now. His hands are clasped behind his back, and he has kept his distance from your sister most faithfully."

"Have you been watching them?" Again, he seemed surprised.

"I have. I would not wish for any ill to befall either my sister or her friend. You are not the only one concerned for a sister's welfare, sir."

He smiled.

"I find myself constantly worrying about Mary now that she has decided to be interested in marrying. It must be doubly difficult for a brother who is charged with the care of his sister."

"Your sister has not always wished to marry?"

"Oh, no, that is not it. She assures me she has always wished to marry. However, she did not wish to be pushed forward so she pretended that she had no desire to marry until she was at least twenty-five."

His eyebrows rose high. "Is that how she has avoided being matched?"

"In part," Elizabeth admitted. "There were other things she did, but I cannot share all her secrets." She glanced to her right and then her left before adding in a whisper, "Not even if the information could be useful to your cousin."

Darcy chuckled. "He is forever attempting to avoid his mother's machinations."

This sort of conversation, where she felt as if she and he were equals and dear friends, was the sort for which she wished. They had spoken like this in the park. "I suspected as much."

He offered her his arm again. "Are you still leaving me?" That peculiar softness that had shone in his eyes the other day was there once again.

She placed her hand on his arm and allowed him to lead her further down the corridor. Mary and Georgiana were just at the end and turning to come back. As she turned, Georgiana's fan which had been dangling from her wrist on a chain fell to the floor. Mr. Hodgkiss was quick in picking it up for her. There was most certainly admiration for Miss Darcy in the gentleman's actions, and from the duck of her head, it appeared the admiration was returned.

"Has your sister met many of your friends?"

"She has met several. Why do you ask?"

"I was wondering if her esteem for Mr. Hodgkiss was because she was inexperienced or if she has evaluated him compared to others. I know she is not out yet, but young ladies do think romantic thoughts even before they are out."

"Yes, I know." His words had taken on a tinge of a cold edge again.

"I did not mean to overstep or offend." Truly, she did not know how her words could have done either, but he had bristled at them.

"You did not." He blew out a breath. "I am just not ready for her to choose anyone." His voice was soft.

"She seems well-prepared. You have done your job well."

He shook his head. "No, I have not, but I intend to fix that."

"How can you say you have not?" Elizabeth asked in surprise. "She has perhaps smiled at Mr. Hodgkiss and ducked her head at his words a few times, but she has been all that is proper and demure. She has not presented herself as one who is openly flirting. She knows her place and how to behave. Would that my youngest sisters were half so restrained as your sister is. You have done well, sir. Whether or not you believe it, I can see it, and so can everyone else."

"I almost lost her to a scoundrel last summer." The words hissed from him and pain etched his handsome features. He moved them to the edge of the hall. "I will not allow that to happen again. I will not fail her." He turned to face her. His lips parted and then closed. He closed his eyes and shook his head as if arguing within himself.

"You did not lose her, and I doubt you are capable of failing her," she whispered.

His eyes opened, and he fixed his gaze on her eyes.

"Miss Darcy is an intelligent young lady. I have seen her ponder things when in conversation with Mary. She will not make the same mistake twice."

"I wish I could believe it," he admitted, taking a step closer to her.

"Do you not trust her?"

"No, that is not it."

"You do not trust Mr. Hodgkiss?"

He shook his head. "I do not know who to trust." This admission was barely above a whisper.

"But you will," she encouraged. It broke her heart to hear the uncertainty in his voice.

"How do you know?"

She shrugged. She was not certain how she knew it, but she did. "I just do."

He grasped her hand. "Then you have more faith in me than I have in myself."

"It is always easier for others to see you than it is for you to see yourself."

His lips tipped into a smile. "I suppose you are correct." He shook his head. "You are both beautiful and wise."

He lifted her hand. Was he going to kiss it? Her heart thudded heavy and hard. First, he said she was beautiful, and now this?

As if he had heard her thoughts and remembered himself, he held her hand in mid-air and bowed over it. "Thank you, Miss Elizabeth. You have been a great help to me." He lowered her hand and releasing it looked around. "Richard," he called upon seeing his cousin.

"How may I be of service?" the colonel asked.

"Would you be so kind as to see that Georgiana and the Miss Bennets are returned home safely? I find I must go home early."

Colonel Fitzwilliam glanced between his cousin and Elizabeth, who shook her head in answer to his unspoken question. She had no idea why Mr. Darcy was suddenly leaving.

"I have a headache starting and fear remaining will only make it worse." He closed his eyes and grimaced as he said it. He was lying, but she did not know why.

"Certainly. I will see them all safely home."

"My carriage is at your disposal."

"No, take it home. Father's carriage has room for us all."

"Thank you," he said to the colonel before turning back to Elizabeth. "Please, accept my sincerest appreciation for sharing your insightful thoughts with me, Miss Elizabeth, and tell your uncle that my sister will be happy to join you for dinner next week. However, I fear I will not be able to attend." He looked away as he said it. "I apologize that I must leave you and your sister before the end of the play."

"Think nothing of it," she assured him, though she would undoubtedly be thinking about it extensively. "A headache is an unpleasant thing." Nearly as unpleasant as a heartache. "I hope it heals quickly with some rest." She also hoped that he was only saying goodbye to her for the night and not forever, though her heart seemed certain he would not be returning.

Chapter 13

Darkness crept into Darcy's study and surrounded everything but the lonely candle on his desk and the glowing embers in the hearth. Darcy sat in one of the wingback chairs that stood before the fire. The heat of the dying embers poked at him and attempted to warm him through, but it was of little use. Darcy's world and all the comforts his station afforded him did nothing to soothe the ache he felt radiating from his heart and piercing every fiber of his being. The port in the glass he held did little to dull the pain. With his free hand, he rubbed the spot between his eyebrows, just above his nose, where a dull pounding insisted on playing its discordant tune. He had hoped a night of rest and a day spent quietly in his study would have improved the condition of his head and heart, but it had not.

He had known he was in danger of losing his heart to Miss Elizabeth. He had just not realized that while he still thought he held it, that traitorous organ had already resigned itself to the lady's control.

He blew out a breath and closed his eyes. Georgiana would be home from visiting Miss Mary soon. He needed to find his resolve so that he could present a convincing all-is-well façade.

The door behind him and to his left opened, and, straightening in his chair, Darcy emptied the contents of his glass.

"Are you doing so poorly that you cannot afford more than one candle? You will do your eyes no favors by attempting to work in such low light."

"I was not working, my lady." Darcy rose to greet his aunt and light a lamp. "What brings you to Darcy House today?"

"You." Lady Matlock took a seat near the fire – or what remained of it. "Are you going to be in here much longer? For if you are, this fire needs tending."

"I am just waiting for Georgiana to return, and then, I will be removing myself to whatever room she chooses."

"Is your headache better?"

"Only slightly," he answered honestly. "My sleep was poor last night, so I am hopeful that tonight will be more restful and restorative."

She tipped her head and studied him for a moment. "You need someone to care for you."

She was not going to begin her refrain of his needing a wife once again, was she? He was certain that his current state of being was not equal to the challenge of tolerating such an onslaught from his aunt.

"I am perfectly capable of caring for myself."

"The circles under your eyes say otherwise."

"I already said I did not sleep well last night. I do not see how anyone could have altered that." Except for him. He could alter all his aches and pains if he would just put his desires ahead of his duty to his sister.

"You missed a very interesting interlude last night."

"Did I?" He eyed her warily. She was not one to give up her attack regarding his need of a wife so easily. He was thankful if she were actually retreating on that front, but he could not help but feel somewhat uneasy at her seeming change of topic.

His aunt nodded. "A gentleman, who we all know but whose name I will not share since that would be far too much like gossip if I did share it."

Darcy was certain that even without giving a name the whole tale was as gossip-like as it could be.

"This gentleman came upon his betrothed at the end of the play just as we were leaving. She had attended with her brother and his wife."

"How is this interesting?" He should not encourage her, but he did wish for her to conclude the tale as quickly as possible.

"Because he was in attendance with another lady. I dare say that betrothal will not survive, and if it does, the marriage will be anything but happy. For you know that a gentleman or lady who is given to disguise and dalliance before marriage does not change simply because they repeated a few vows. They should, but you know they do not."

"Yes, I have heard you say that many times."

"So you have been listening to me!" She cried brightly.

"At times."

Lady Matlock chuckled. "Most likely more often than my sons do."

Darcy shook his head. "I doubt it. I am just more willing to admit to having listened."

"And less prone to provoke."

"Yes, and less prone to that." Both of his cousins loved nothing better than to needle their mother.

"Richard went to Gracechurch Street today with Georgiana."

"Yes, I know." Darcy had been grateful for his cousin's willingness to attend Georgiana and Mrs. Annesley on their call today.

"I asked him to invite Miss Elizabeth and Miss Mary to Matlock House. I like them quite well, you know."

"I know." He kept his answer short because he did not want to hear her elaborate on what she liked about Miss Mary and Miss Elizabeth. Indeed, he had been attempting to ignore all the lovely things he admired about Miss Elizabeth. Not that he had succeeded. But he had tried.

"I would be quite happy to have either of my boys marry one or the other of the Bennet sisters I have met."

And they were back to the topic of marriage –

which he had no desire to discuss. However, if he did not say something about it, his aunt would press to know why he was avoiding the topic rather than putting up some argument against it. "The Miss Bennets have very little to add to a marriage by way of standing or income."

Her eyes grew wide, and she wore an affronted look. Apparently, she more than sort of liked Miss Mary and Miss Elizabeth.

"They have all that is needed to add to a marriage," she said sharply. "Caring hearts, excellent characters, fine manners, intelligent minds."

Oh, he knew that quite well. Miss Elizabeth was every one of those things and more. "But you know what Richard says."

"My son says a lot of things. About half of them are true, and if I know him so well as I think I do, money will not be the first qualification of which he makes note when selecting a bride. He is more like you in that regard than you might realize. You both wish for love and a wife who is more than a milquetoast maid without an original thought in her pretty head."

"I will allow that you might be right about that."

"Whether you allow it or not, I am right."

Darcy chuckled. His aunt was always convinced she was right until it became obvious that she might not be, and even then, it could take some time before she was willing to admit defeat.

"And that is why I am truly here."

Darcy cocked an eyebrow. "What do you mean?"

"I meant what I said when I said I would not mind having either Miss Bennet as a daughter. However, Miss Mary seems enamored with Mr. Pointon – who would be an excellent choice. And I had thought her sister to be quite lost to you. However, she and Richard did seem to enjoy one another's company after you left last night, so if you do not plan to pursue the lady, I had thought to point her in Richard's direction."

Richard and Miss Elizabeth? The thought settled onto Darcy like a villain intent upon snuffing out his life with a pillow.

"Are... are you certain they would suit?" He only just resisted the urge to loosen his cravat.

"Oh, I am never certain of a match until I have seen the couple together a few times. A gentleman and a lady could look very well together on first meeting, but then as one gets to see the gentleman flinch in annoyance at something the lady does or says, or the lady insists upon fluttering her lashes at other gentlemen despite having her hand on her gentleman's arm..." she shrugged. "You see how it can be, do you not?"

Darcy was not sure he did, but he was not about to ask for clarification. Therefore, he nodded as if what she had said was perfectly logical, and knowing his aunt, it likely was. It was just that his mind was not functioning as it should at present.

"I just need to know that I will not be setting you against Richard."

Again, he nodded as if his mind could fully comprehend what she was saying. "Can you not just allow Richard to find his own wife?"

"Do you not think that Richard and Miss Elizabeth would suit?"

He was surely going to expire right there in the chair in his study. She wanted him to not just allow for her to promote the match but for him to approve of it as well? How was he supposed to offer up the holder of his heart to another? Of course, she would eventually find a husband, and it could happen before he was prepared to seek a wife. He would dearly love to ask his father right now why a

Darcy had to do his duty before he could take his ease.

"How should I know?" If he could just avoid giving his approval of the match…

"You have spent more time with Miss Elizabeth than I have, and you know your cousin."

He closed his eyes. "I will not give my approval to a scheme to push Richard in any direction." He opened his eyes to find her smiling at him. It was unnerving. She should not be smiling at his refusal.

"That is good to hear." She placed her hands on the arms of the chair and pushed to her feet, and Darcy rose with her.

"We will be joining Mr. Bingley at Netherfield for Christmas," she said as she moved around her chair to the back of it as if preparing to leave. "I have agreed to serve as his hostess. He and your uncle came to the agreement last night while you were walking in the hall."

"I had thought to invite you to join us here."

"Oh." Her eyebrows rose high. "Did Georgiana not tell you?"

"I have not seen her today."

"I suppose that would explain a thing or two."

"What was my sister to tell me?"

"You and she are joining us at Netherfield. It is your uncle's gift to Georgie that she gets to spend her Christmas with her friend, and now that I know you do not mind if I promote Miss Elizabeth to Richard –"

"I did not say that," Darcy protested.

"I know you did not, but you also did not discourage me from it either. Therefore, I will have your uncle insist that Richard joins us for Christmas. It will help keep that horrid fellow, Mr. Wickham, in check if he is still there."

"What do you mean if he is still there?"

"Your uncle has some plans, but I am not at liberty to discuss them."

Darcy felt a bit as if he was at sea on the rolling ocean – unsteady and quite nauseated. His aunt was going to try to match Richard with Elizabeth, and he was going to have to be in attendance while it happened? He shook his head. He could not do that. "I cannot go to Netherfield for Christmas."

"I do not see why you cannot."

"I just cannot."

"You would let Georgiana spend Christmas without you?"

He blew out a breath, willing his head to stop spinning and longing for the room to stop swaying. "I would rather she spend it in town with me, but I do not see how that is going to be possible." Darcy grasped the back of the chair in which he had been sitting.

"Fitzwilliam," Georgiana stopped just inside the door to his study. "Are you well?"

He nodded, though he knew it was a lie. His heart was beating even though it felt as if it was dying.

"His head is still not well," Lady Matlock said to Georgiana. "Do sit down, Fitzwilliam. You do not need to stand on my account. I was just telling him, Georgie, that you will be joining us for Christmas at Netherfield."

Darcy did as instructed and returned to his seat.

"Is that why he is unwell?" Richard teased from where he leaned against the door frame.

"I suppose it could be since I also told him that you would be accompanying us."

"Me?"

"Yes, you. You are my son and Georgiana's guardian. Who else would I wish to take with us?

Now, tell me. How was your visit at Gracechurch Street? Did you have tea with Miss Gardiner?"

"Yes, we did, and Master Gardiner joined us as well," Georgiana answered, though she was still looking at Darcy with concern. "I met the other two Gardiner children today. Albert is nearly three and simply adorable, and Nicholas is not yet one. He scoots around the floor but has not yet learned to walk, though he does pull himself up on things."

"Miss Gardiner insisted on showing Georgie the nursery. It is well-appointed. Gardiner does not seem to lack for money," Richard added. "They even have two nursemaids." He came over and claimed the chair his mother had vacated.

"Where are we to sit?" his mother teased.

"In the drawing room as is proper," Richard retorted.

Lady Matlock laughed. "Come along, Georgie. The men would like to be alone."

"Not before I give Fitzwilliam his gift."

"You have a gift for me?" Darcy asked.

Georgiana sat down on the footstool in front of him. "It is not from me. It is from Miss Gardiner, and do not worry, her brother lectured her most severely about giving gifts to gentlemen."

"Aye, that he did," Richard said with a laugh. "Not that it was going to stop the young miss. She said that you were Miss Darcy's brother and, therefore, not a gentleman."

Darcy chuckled. "And how did Master Gardiner reply to that?"

"He did not, for his mother did not allow it," Richard said. "She, however, assured Miss Gardiner that you were indeed a gentleman, and that there was nothing improper if she gave you a gift with her mother's and father's permission."

Georgiana placed a painting of a large yellow blotch on his lap. "Miss Gardiner had heard you left the play early last night because you were not well, so she made you some sunshine that she promises will not make your head hurt more. That way if you have to lie in bed with the curtains drawn, you will still have something bright and cheery to make you feel better." She pointed to a red blob at the bottom of the painting that was surrounded by green. "That is a flower because they smell pretty and make her smile."

"She is a dear, is she not?" Lady Matlock said.

"She is," Georgiana agreed. "She told me that

she was going to paint one for her cousin tomorrow."

Darcy's head tipped. "Which cousin?"

"Miss Elizabeth."

"Is she ill?"

Georgiana shook her head. "She was just not herself today. She seemed a bit melancholy."

He picked up the painting Miss Gardiner had made him and studied it, choosing to focus on it rather than the longing to inquire after Miss Elizabeth's melancholy.

His sister rose and gave him a kiss on his forehead. "Would you like me to play for you later?"

He nodded. "I would like that."

"Do you think your head can endure it?"

"If you play soothing music, I think so." And his heart needed it.

Chapter 14

Mary sat down at the instrument in Matlock House's music room and placed her fingers on the keys. Georgiana stood ready to move the sheets of music as needed.

Lady Matlock leaned close to Elizabeth and whispered. "It is always such a pleasure to have someone play for me. It is a vastly different experience to listen without having to remember which keys to hit at what time."

"Do you play often?" Elizabeth asked as she tried to picture Lady Matlock at the piano.

"I would like to play daily, but life does not always make that possible."

The first notes of the song Mary had been working on rang out in the room. Her playing, just like her appearance and disposition, had taken on a wholly different air. In town, she allowed herself to feel the emotion of the music. Here, she was no longer attempting to put off her mother or appear to be less than what any gentleman might want as a wife. Here, she was blossoming and becoming a proper and appealing young lady. Even with her heart feeling as if it had been ground to dust by a millstone, Elizabeth could not and would not regret her time in town simply because it had given Mary her moment to discover who she wanted to be. Who Elizabeth wanted to be had also been discovered, but it was never to be attained.

"Do you play or is it just your sister who does?" Lady Matlock asked. "She is doing well. A bit more practice and she will shine, absolutely shine."

It lifted Elizabeth's spirits to hear her sister praised for an accomplishment. Would not Mama be delighted to hear her daughter commended by the Countess of Matlock? That is, she would be delighted after she got over the shock of the fact that it was Mary who was being commended and not Jane or Lydia.

"I do play, but my playing is not so good as Mary's is. It is most likely because I do not practice as I should."

Lady Matlock chuckled. "I admire your honesty.

Will you demonstrate your ability or lack thereof for me?"

"Only if I am forced. I am sure I would look like a very poor student indeed with three ladies in the room who can play far better than I."

"I did not say I play well," Lady Matlock replied.

"You do not play well?" Had she not just said she would like to play daily? Would that not make her an excellent pianist?

"I play from my heart and sometimes my heart causes my fingers to stumble in its exuberance over the swells and strains of the piece." She smirked. "Not even practising so much as I do has fixed my inability to make it though a simple piece without fudging and fumbling. Still, I persist, for I am not easily thwarted. You and your sister strike me as being similar to me in that regard. I dare say you are one to not be swayed from your position without a bit of effort, and from what I have seen of Miss Mary, I would say she is even more of a challenge to depose."

Elizabeth laughed. "Obstinacy is not in short supply at my home."

"That is not so bad a thing if a lady's headstrong nature is directed at the right things. For instance, my stubbornness was and is needed to survive my children. Richard is as immovable as a cranky old donkey at times. His brother is only slightly less stubborn, and you have met my nephew. He can be quite determined that he is correct, even when he is not. Your cousin, Master Gardiner, seems to be cut from the same cloth as my nephew." She smiled as if remembering something. "He reminds me a great deal of Fitzwilliam when he was a boy." She shook her head. "The number of times Fitzwilliam had to stop and redo what he was doing..." She laughed softly to herself. "He grew up to be a fine gentleman, however. Would you not agree?"

Oh, why did she have to talk about Mr. Darcy? Elizabeth forced a smile to her face. "I am sure I have not met a gentleman who is better."

Lady Matlock's eyebrows rose. "Indeed? I had thought you might have given up on him."

Heat flooded Elizabeth's face. "Given up on him? I was never pursuing him." She was hoping he might come to love her, but she had not tried to draw him along.

"I did not mean you were pursuing. I meant that I thought you might admire him."

"Oh." Elizabeth did not know how else to

respond to such a statement. She did not just admire him. She loved him. She blinked against the tears that gathered at the thought. She would not cry here. She would not. She would wait until she was tucked in bed. Then, with darkness hiding her sorrow, she would allow it to escape. The music room at Matlock House was not the proper place to dissolve into tears, especially when she could feel Lady Matlock's eyes observing her.

"Do you sing, Miss Elizabeth?"

"Yes, I do." She was certain she had never been happier for a change of topic.

"Then, you may choose which accomplishment you prefer to display for me: your singing or your playing." She lifted a hand to signal Georgiana as the song Mary was playing drew to a close. "Miss Elizabeth must have a turn next," she instructed before turning back to Elizabeth. "Which will it be? Singing or playing?"

"I suppose I shall sing?" Was that the best choice? Her voice was not dreadful, though it was not the sort that people paid to listen to at a concert hall either. It was easier to perform a piece vocally than to play anything without stumbling. Therefore, it was the right choice, was it not?

"Oh! What will you sing, Lizzy?" Mary asked eagerly. "I love listening to her sing," she told Lady Matlock.

"You do?" Elizabeth had never seen any evidence of it. Mary had always appeared bored when listening to anyone sing.

"I could not let Mama know that I enjoyed it."

"Why ever not? I do not see how that could have caused Mama to put your forward when you did not wish it."

Mary's brow furrowed. "I suppose you are correct, but I have admitted it was perhaps not the best-thought-out scheme."

Lady Matlock looked between the two of them. "I admit to being consumed with curiosity. What scheme is this?"

Elizabeth was sure her eyes were as wide as Mary's. In her surprise over Mary's admission to liking to listen to her sing, Elizabeth had forgotten that Miss Darcy and her aunt did not know about Mary's change from who she had been in Hertfordshire to who she was now.

"I apologize Mary. I was not thinking."

"Think nothing of it. The whole thing is going to be revealed when we get home. I might as well confess to it now, especially since Lady Matlock and Georgiana will be joining us in Hertfordshire for Christmas."

"This is only making me more curious," Lady Matlock said.

"Me, too," Georgiana added.

Mary took a seat next to Georgiana on a settee to Lady Matlock's left. "Do you remember that I said it is possible to avoid being matched, my lady?"

"Indeed, I do, though I expressed my doubts about the possibility."

"It is entirely possible," Mary assured her. "I have done it quite successfully. At home, before I came to town, I dressed like a spinster. I swore I was not going to marry until I was twenty-five and then, only if I was unable to set up my own establishment or find employment I could tolerate. I complained loudly about having to dance. I read sermons – sometimes out loud to my sisters – and I quoted scripture and lectured. I taught myself to play the piano in a fashion that was technically correct but never heart-felt – that was not easy."

"Oh, my." Lady Matlock seemed to be at a loss for words.

"Such oddities were too much for my mother to overcome, and so she left me alone."

"How long did you keep up this charade?" Lady Matlock asked.

"Three and a half years. I only just recently, when I began to long for a husband and family of my own, decided that it was a dreadful plan."

"Three and a half years?" Lady Matlock stared at Mary in disbelief.

"Yes, my lady."

"How did you do it?" Georgiana's question was filled with incredulity. "I am sure I could never pretend something for so long."

"It actually was only hard at first and then at last. The middle part where Mama was ignoring me in favour of putting forward my sisters was the easy bit." She looked at Elizabeth. "I am so very grateful for this trip to town for giving me a place to change and for my sister's help in making the changes I needed to make."

"I do not believe I have ever met anyone, gentleman or lady, who has such resolve," Lady Matlock said. "I am impressed. I suppose your transformation will come as quite the shock to your mother."

Mary nodded. "I am sure it will. However, she

will likely just think it was clever of my father to have sent me to town, and I suspect she will be eager to send me back to town since this trip wrought such wonders."

Lady Matlock laughed and not lightly. Her laugh was a deep, all-encompassing laugh. "Delightful! Simply delightful." She said when she could finally speak again.

"You do not find it to be a serious character flaw that I practiced such deception?" Mary looked anxiously at Georgiana. "I have been considering how wrong it was of me to be so deceitful. I promise I have repented of it in my prayers every night."

Georgiana placed a hand on top of Mary's folded ones. "We all make errors. Some are longer than others, but that does not mean they are greater." She glanced at her aunt and then Elizabeth. "I made a grave error last summer and almost eloped with a gentleman who claimed to love me. However, he did not. He loved my money and wished to harm my brother since Fitzwilliam had refused to give him the living my father had left him in his will." She shook her head. "But he had already refused the living and accepted money in its stead from my brother."

"How dreadful," Mary said. "Not that you nearly eloped," she hurried to clarify, "but that a gentleman would be so scheming."

"You will not tell anyone, will you?"

"Never." The word sprang from Elizabeth's lips only seconds before Mary said the same thing.

"He is the reason my brother did not want to go to Netherfield for Christmas because he is in Hertfordshire with the militia."

A vivid memory came to the forefront of Elizabeth's memory. "Mr. Wickham?" she asked in a whisper.

Georgiana blinked. "Yes, but how did you know?"

"The day before Mary and I left for town, my sisters and I met Mr. Wickham in Meryton, and we were speaking to him when Mr. Bingley and your brother came upon us. The look on your brother's face..." The greeting or, more precisely, the lack thereof between the two gentlemen made a great deal of sense in the light of what Miss Darcy had revealed. "I thought your brother was just being rude again." She shrugged. "Apparently, he was not."

"What do you mean by *rude again?*" Lady Matlock inquired.

"Mr. Darcy said something at the assembly he attended when he first arrived in Meryton. It was unkind." Oh, she did not wish to get into this. "He has since apologized." It was not as if he had asked her forgiveness in words, but he had shown himself to be sorry in his actions that day at Darcy House when she, Mary, and her aunt had had tea there.

"He said something unkind to you?" Lady Matlock seemed to be struggling to comprehend the concept.

"Not to me, but about me, and I heard it. I do not think he knew I had heard it until recently."

"I am surprised," Georgiana said, "but he was not happy to leave me. He worries so much about me. He always has, even before Father died. And then, I had made just made such a foolish mistake." She sighed. "It still weighs on him, especially with my season only a year away."

"That is understandable." So much about Mr. Darcy and how he behaved was beginning to fall neatly into place. Of course, he was in an ill-humor when he was in Hertfordshire. Of course, he would be overly critical of anyone who dared to show preference – even properly – for his sister. "I worry about my sisters, too."

"I fear he takes it too far." Georgiana smiled sadly at Elizabeth as if there was some connection between Mr. Darcy's worry for his sister and her, but it was a connection she could not decipher.

"He is a bright boy. He will figure it out," Lady Matlock assured Georgiana. "Now, what will Miss Elizabeth sing for us while we wait for some refreshment, for I intend to ring for some." She leaned forward and whispered, "I am quite beside myself with wanting some gingerbread." She winked. "And that should bring me some company from my youngest son as gingerbread is his favourite." She stood. "Could I make a small request?" She directed the question to Elizabeth.

"Of course."

"Would you please sing a Christmas song?"

"If you have some that I know."

"Oh!" Mary cried. "I saw 'The Holly and The Ivy' in the folder. It is one of your favourites."

Elizabeth rose to follow Mary and Miss Darcy to the piano. "How can I resist a favourite, though

I had not realized you knew it was one of my favourites."

"You always pick that one first, and you leave off reading to listen when I play it – even when I was not playing it well."

"Then, you must play it while Miss Elizabeth sings," Georgiana inserted.

Delight suffused Mary's features. "Could I sing with you?" she asked eagerly.

"Of course, you may."

"I promise to sing it as prettily as I can and not how I might normally do."

Elizabeth linked arms with Mary and chuckled. "I find the new Mary delightful, especially since I can still see some of the old Mary in her." She squeezed Mary's arm and whispered. "I love both of them." But she loved most that it seemed her sister loved the new Mary, too, and that was the love on which she would focus her mind instead of the one she had lost when Mr. Darcy had left the theatre.

Chapter 15

"I am to inform the colonel," Matlock House's butler said from the door to the billiard's room, "that my lady is serving gingerbread to her guests."

"Are they still in the music room?" Richard put his cue on the table and turned toward the door.

Darcy shook his head. Lady Matlock knew how to gain her son's attention, and to gain it quickly. She just needed to mention a favourite treat and he was off. It had been so since he was a boy.

"Yes, sir, they are."

"Are you joining me?" Richard asked Darcy.

"No." As much as he would love to have some tea and something sweet, that would defeat his plan for the afternoon, for it would be much harder to avoid Miss Elizabeth while sitting in the same room with her.

"You cannot hide from her forever unless you forbid Georgiana to be friends with Miss Mary."

That was true. But... "I can hide for now."

Richard sighed, and Darcy knew his cousin wished to launch into the same lecture he had given Darcy yesterday. However, it did not matter what Richard said. Darcy knew that he had to keep his distance from Miss Elizabeth if he was going to keep his focus where it needed to be – with Georgiana.

Elizabeth. He shook his head. Miss Elizabeth was distracting. Terribly distracting. She made him think of marrying, and that was not something he could consider until he had seen to his duty in seeing Georgiana well-settled.

"You are being ridiculous," Richard muttered.

"I am not. I am doing what my father taught me. *A Darcy sees to his duty before he seeks pleasure.*"

"I still say you are being foolish," Richard said before leaving the room.

Darcy moved Richard's cue from the table and began a solitary game. Music drifted down the hall from the music room. Richard must have left the door open there just as he had in this room. If there was one thing which his cousin had always disliked, it was being closed in. He liked being able to keep an eye on all that was happening around him. Therefore, leaving a door open gave him an opportunity to hear and see what passed in the corridor.

Darcy paused his playing and went to the door to listen. A familiar sweet voice carried the words of a favourite Christmas song to him. Miss Elizabeth was singing, but she was not singing alone. Was that Miss Mary? It was not Georgiana. The right side of his mouth tipped into a half-smile. Miss Mary's voice was nearly as beautiful as Miss Elizabeth's. He rested against the door frame and closed his eyes as he listened.

"You could enjoy the music better in the music room."

Darcy jumped at his uncle's words.

"My apologies. I did not mean to startle you."

"I did not hear you approach." Darcy pushed off the door frame.

His uncle, who was at his side, clapped him on the shoulder. "We must talk."

It was not a request. Darcy could hear the demand in his uncle's tone.

"Is something wrong?" he asked as he followed his uncle down the corridor.

"In my opinion and that of my wife, yes." He stopped at the door to the music room. "That was lovely," he said as he poked his head into the room.

Darcy listened as both Miss Mary and Miss Elizabeth thanked him.

"Are you joining us?" his aunt asked.

"No. I have something to discuss with Fitzwilliam."

It was never a good sign when his uncle started calling him by his Christian name. Darcy's mind began whirling as he tried to reason out what he might have done to earn the appellation of Fitzwilliam instead of Darcy from his uncle. Perhaps it was because he was refusing to go to Netherfield.

There was a rustling of skirts, and his aunt appeared at the door with a small plate containing two gingerbreads. "I cannot have you going without."

"Thank you, my dear." He placed a kiss on her cheek. "We will be in my study."

And again, Darcy was following behind his uncle like a schoolboy who was in trouble.

"Beside the fire," his uncle said as he crossed the room to the cabinet where he kept the brandy he favoured. "Do you care for a glass to go with your gingerbread?"

"Please." Darcy attempted to settle into his chair as if he were just visiting his uncle at any other time, but he could not. He had always disliked being called into his father's study to discuss some bit of trouble.

His uncle brought the brandy over first and then, placed the plate of gingerbreads on the table between the two chairs.

"What have I done?" Darcy asked before his uncle could even sit down.

Lord Matlock chuckled. "Why do you think you have done something?"

"Because you said that something was wrong, and then, you used my Christian name."

His uncle took up his glass of brandy and swirled it, watching the liquid rise and fall as he spoke. "What do you think you have done?"

This was the worst way for a discussion to begin. For, all the discussions between him and his father which had started this way had always ended with his father knowing about more sins than he had when Darcy had first entered the study. He drew a breath. He might as well make his admissions and have it over with.

"I do not plan to go to Netherfield for Christmas."

"Yes, that will not do. You will be with us." His uncle leveled a severe glare at him. "You will not be absent for Georgiana's Christmas. Why, she may meet new acquaintances – even gentlemen when she is in Hertfordshire. Is it not your duty to see that her friendships are acceptable?"

"Richard will be there. He is her guardian just as much as I am."

"Indeed." His uncle's eyebrows rose over another pointed look, which was likely supposed to mean something, though Darcy had no idea what it was. When Darcy did not respond, Lord Matlock continued. "You do not know how many Christmases you may have left with your sister. Once she has married, she may spend them with her husband's family. She will be out next season. If she is successful, you may only have this Christmas and next. Therefore, to save you from the regret you will feel, I am going to insist that you spend Christmas with us at Netherfield."

Darcy looked down into his glass. "I had not

considered that." He could very well be alone in two years' time. Alone. That thought did not settle well on him. If he married… no, that would not do.

"I figured as much. You are not one to shirk your duty unless you have a good reason or are not thinking clearly."

His uncle was accusing him of shirking his duty? He took a slow sip of his brandy and accepted the gingerbread his uncle offered him.

"Now, to the reason why I really wished to speak with you."

Of course, it was as he had suspected. He had just earned himself a reprimand for something that he likely would not have if he had kept silent. However, he was not sorry he had heard his uncle's thoughts about Netherfield. He was actually glad to have his thinking altered. He would just have to devise a way to avoid Miss Elizabeth so much as he was able to while at Netherfield.

"Your sister tells me that you agreed to partake in the festivities at Gracechurch Street with her."

Darcy nodded as his brow furrowed. What could his uncle have to say about that? He had not had any issue with visiting the Gardiners and had since that visit, mentioned just how much he liked them.

"And yet, you have refused an invitation to dinner next Monday and are sending her by herself – or with Richard, who made no such promise." His uncle placed his brandy on the table. "I am not going to tell you again that you are disappointing your sister."

"You are not?"

Lord Matlock shook his head. "I will not say that I am happy that you are disappointing her, but I am even more grieved that you are not keeping your word to a very sweet young girl, who painted you a picture and was nearly in tears to hear that not all of her new friends were coming to the special dinner. And, it sets a poor example for young Master Gardiner to see someone of your rank showing such contempt for a promise."

"I am not showing contempt for a promise. Just because I said I would take part in some of the festivities does not mean I can be part of all of them."

"Does it not? Is it not your duty to keep your word?"

"Yes, but..." He shook his head. "I cannot attend."

"Do you have a previous engagement?"

Darcy swallowed. "No."

"Then, you are declining the invitation because you do not want to go."

He wanted to plead that it was not a want but a need that kept him from attending the dinner, but he could not. His uncle was correct. It was desire alone that kept him from accepting the Gardiner's invitation.

He nodded as shame washed over him.

"I am certain you know what to do."

He did. He would have to write to Mr. Gardiner and tell him that he would be attending dinner on Monday if the invitation was still open. He discarded his glass of brandy in favour of eating his gingerbread. How was he going to deny his desire to present himself as a suitor to Miss Elizabeth when they would be together in such an intimate setting?

"Your father was a good man, Fitzwilliam."

"I know."

"And I know you have always wished to please him, and you have succeeded until now." His uncle rose to return to the bottle of brandy that stood on the cabinet across the study. "Duty should always be considered when making decisions, but to be the man your father hoped you would be, you must learn to blend duty with pleasure. Your father tended to Pemberley and his family with vigor. No one could accuse him of being anything other than a proper master, husband, and father."

Darcy smiled. That described his father perfectly.

"But," his uncle turned to face him, "he never once denied himself the joy of being your mother's husband or yours and Georgiana's father. At times, I know he likely said he could not play with you or look at whatever you wished to show him because he had a tenant to visit, a field to view, or an account to balance, but once the pressing task was completed, he found time to spend with you and your sister – and your mother when she was alive. In fact, her wishes always came before anyone else's." He smiled softly. "I could not have asked for a better husband for my sister. I know she was loved as deeply as any lady could be loved."

He crossed the room just as the door opened and his wife entered.

"Georgiana is ready to go home. The Miss Bennets have already left."

Darcy washed the last morsel of his gingerbread

down with what was left of his brandy and then rose to leave.

"Fitzwilliam," his uncle called to him before he left the room.

"I know what I must do."

Lord Matlock shook his head. "That was not what I was going to say. I was going to ask you if you knew why your father left Georgiana's care to both you and Richard?"

"To keep a tie to her mother's family." That is what his father had said when he had presented the idea to Darcy a few years before his death.

"That is one reason, but it is not the only reason."

"Is it not? Then, what is the rest of the reason?"

"He named you both because he knew that seeing to a duty so vital as helping a young girl become a young lady is often easier when one has help." He lifted his glass and smiled. "Even if that help is my troublesome and opinionated son. Take care on the way home. It has begun snowing."

~*~*~

Three days later, Darcy stood outside the Gardiner's house next to his sister, waiting for the door to open. He blew out a breath and watched it float away on the breeze.

"You seem nervous to be here," Georgiana said.

He rubbed his hands together. "I am."

"Why?"

"I must set a few things right."

He had spent hours pondering his conversation with his uncle, and he had come to an important conclusion. Richard had been right when he said Darcy was being both ridiculous and foolish, and his uncle had made a very good point when he said that Darcy's father had never placed Darcy's mother second to duty. The two – duty and Darcy's mother – had been nearly equal in importance to his father, but as Darcy had recalled many memories from his youth, he had come to realize that, for his father, duty had never come before his wife or his family.

"With Miss Elizabeth?" Georgiana's excitement was not well disguised.

He nodded.

The door before them opened, and Darcy blew out one more breath before stepping into the house.

"Mr. Darcy!" Miss Gardiner cried in delight when he entered the sitting room behind his sister.

Miss Elizabeth's eyes went wide at the sight of him, and her cheeks flushed rosy as he held her gaze.

"Please, be seated," Mr. Gardiner offered.

Darcy was glad that Elizabeth's uncle was home. It would make for less repeating of his errors.

"May I speak before I sit?" he asked.

Mr. Gardiner's brow furrowed. "Of course."

"I find myself needing to correct my actions."

Master Gardiner's head tipped at that.

"I refused a most gracious invitation for no good reason. I would be honored to be a guest at your table on Monday if I am still allowed to be."

"There is always room at our table," Mr. Gardiner said with a smile.

"I apologize that my refusal brought you sadness, Miss Gardiner, and I must thank you for your lovely painting. I plan to hang it in my study because sometimes calculating sums can be dreary work." There was still a painting Georgiana had made for her father hanging in the study at Pemberley.

"That is so lovely of you to do," Mrs. Gardiner

dabbed at her eyes while her daughter's face was overcome with a smile, and delight of the purest sort shone in her eyes.

"And now to my not-so-good reason for refusing your invitation." He looked at Elizabeth. This was going to be the hardest piece. "I was scared."

Miss Gardiner gasped.

"Of what?" Master Gardiner asked.

He fixed his eyes on Master Gardiner. "Of love."

There were several gasps from the females in the room, but young Martin Gardiner only looked at him in confusion. "Why would that scare you?"

"Why, indeed." He laughed lightly. "I did say it was not a good reason, did I not?"

The lad nodded.

"I was afraid that allowing myself to love a very pretty and kind young lady would keep me from doing my duty to my sister and making sure she was safe."

Master Gardiner nodded as if he understood. "Sisters are trouble," he said very seriously.

"I am not trouble," Miss Gardiner declared.

"No, you are not trouble," Darcy assured her, "nor is my sister – at least, not in the way you may be thinking. But in a worrying sort of way. Neither your brother nor I would want anything bad to happen to our sisters."

Again, Master Gardiner nodded. "A troubled mind – is that not what you call it, Mama?"

"That is it precisely. Did you wish to speak to one of my pretty nieces in private, Mr. Darcy?" Mrs. Gardiner said.

Darcy allowed himself to look once again at Elizabeth, who was covering her lips with her hand but appeared to be smiling. That was a good sign, was it not? "If she and her uncle will allow it."

"You have my permission," her uncle answered readily. "Elizabeth, you may speak to Mr. Darcy in the dining room."

Darcy held his hand out to her. "Please?"

She placed her hand in his and allowed him to first help her from her seat and then to lead her down the short hall to the dining room. Those were also good signs, he told himself in an attempt to slow his rapidly beating heart.

"Allow me to begin by telling you that I have been a fool."

She said not a word, but her eyes were not silent. They were speaking all that was in her heart. She would not send him away.

"And allow me to continue by saying I love you. Against my will, you have claimed my heart, and I am pleased to let you keep it, if you will have it and me."

Her hand rested on her heart. "What are you asking me?" The question was barely above a whisper.

"Will you marry me? I know we do not know each other so well as some might before they come to an understanding, but –"

"Yes," she said, interrupting his babbling.

"You will?" She would accept him so easily as that?

"Yes," she repeated. "I have known for some days now that I love you."

"You do?" The joy he felt in his heart scrawled itself across his face in what was most assuredly the silliest grin he had ever worn.

"I do." She took a step towards him. "Mary told me that magic was possible at Christmas time. I allowed that it might be true just to encourage her." She shook her head as she smiled up at him. "But she must be right, for my greatest wish stands before me."

"And my greatest desire stands before me." He

took her hand and pulled her to him. "May I kiss you, Elizabeth?"

She nodded, and he lowered his head to press his lips to hers as he wound his arms around her and her arms encircled his neck. One kiss became two and then three and four before a knock at the door and her uncle's clearing of his throat parted them.

Darcy allowed her to step back from him, and when she reached for his hand, he knew to the bottom of his soul that he would forever be grateful that he was dreadful at planning escapes. For if he had not fled Netherfield, he would never have been given her, his greatest gift and his little bit of the magic that could be found, woven in the joy and love, that was Christmas in Gracechurch Street.

Before You Go

If you enjoyed this book, be sure to let others know by leaving a review.

~*~*~

Want to know when other books in this series will be available?

You can always know what's new with my books by subscribing to my mailing list.

(There will, of course, be a thank you gift for joining because I think my readers are awesome!)

Book News from Leenie Brown

(bit.ly/LeenieBBookNews)

~*~*~

Turn the page to read an excerpt from another one of Leenie's books

Two Days Before Christmas Excerpt

[*Do you enjoy Christmas romances featuring Darcy and Elizabeth? Then, allow me to recommend Two Days Before Christmas and share an excerpt from the first chapter with you.*]

Chapter 1

Georgiana Darcy peered out her bedroom window to see who had come to call and was causing the flurry of activity in the halls. Her eyes grew wide as she saw her brother step down from his travelling coach and give some directives to a footman — likely about his trunk or possibly requesting tea. Those were the things he most often thought of first when arriving home from a trip. Her brows furrowed, and her lips pinched into a displeased pucker. Her brother was not supposed to be here in town. He was supposed to be in Hertfordshire with Mr. Bingley, learning how to be something other than unpleasant.

Honestly! It was her heart that had been broken by that cad Wickham, not his! Hers was mending, but his? She shook her head. If only she could do something to prove to him that, though she had been hurt — and grievously so –, her heart was no longer affected. In fact, she had recently begun to think that it had never actually been touched at all. She had not been in love with Wickham. She was nearly convinced of that fact. She had been in love with the idea of being loved, adored, and cherished by a handsome man. That she had not been and feared she might never be was what still caused a pinching pain in her heart. Her companion, Mrs. Annesley, assured her it was a foolish notion to judge every gentleman by the actions of one, but it seemed prudent to Georgiana to be cautious, just in case. She had been too trusting. No one could tell her otherwise. However, just because she needed to learn a lesson in prudence, did not mean her brother needed to continue to suffer. He had done precisely as he should. Her pain was not his doing. The fact that he still tormented himself with guilt was what made it nearly impossible for her to lay her own, well-deserved, shame aside.

She had spoken in confidence about such things to Mr. Bingley before he and her brother had departed for Netherfield, Mr. Bingley's new estate. He had promised he would do his best to see her brother engaged in activities that would bring him distraction if not pleasure. She had been so hopeful that Mr. Bingley had been successful, for Fitzwilliam's letters had been light in tone, sharing stories of the various people he had met and wishing he was free of the attentions of one particular person, Caroline Bingley. Added to that, yesterday, Mr. Bingley had called to inform her that her brother had done the most unusual thing by dancing with a Miss Elizabeth — the same Miss Elizabeth that had featured in more than one of Fitzwilliam's missives.

Why he was home when things had seemed so promising, she was uncertain. She grabbed a wrap for her shoulders and slipped her feet into her slippers.

"Your brother has returned," Mrs. Annesley said as Georgiana met her in the corridor.

"I saw his carriage," Georgiana replied. "It is very unexpected."

"It is," Mrs. Annesley agreed. "Do you wish for me to attend you?"

Georgiana shook her head.

Mrs. Annesley glanced down the stairs. "You will tell me how he is, will you not?" There was a note of worry in her whispered question.

As far as Georgiana was concerned, hiring Mrs. Annesley to be her companion was the best gift Fitzwilliam had ever given her. Mrs. Annesley's heart was far softer than her angular features and austere manner of dress suggested. She was also aware of far more than the spectacles that perched on her nose while she read and stitched might indicate.

"Of course, I will," Georgiana assured her.

A twinkle shone in the lady's eye. "Then be quick."

Georgiana giggled as she descended the stairs. Mrs. Annesley was quiet and reserved as was proper for one in her position, but she was also curious and lively when she and Georgiana were alone. Reaching the bottom of the stairs, Georgiana stopped and waited patiently as her brother removed his outerwear and apologized to Mr. Wright, his butler, for the unexpected change in plans.

Seeing her, he greeted her first with a smile and then open arms, which she ran into without a second's pause.

"I have missed you," he murmured against her hair before releasing her.

"You did not return on my account, did you?" Georgiana wrapped her arm around his.

"May I not wish to see my sister?"

His avoidance of her question was not a good sign. Such a tactic always meant he did not wish to discuss his reasons for something.

"You may wish to see her, but you should not do so at the expense of breaking your word to a friend." She felt his arm flinch. "Mr. Bingley called on me yesterday. He seemed eager to return to Hertfordshire." Again, his arm flinched.

"He may return anytime he wishes."

Her brows drew together. Her brother's tone was so flat, so uncaring — so very unlike him. "I assume Miss Bingley and the Hursts accompanied you back to town?"

"They did."

She lifted a brow and gave him an assessing look. "You know Mr. Bingley will never persuade Caroline away from town so close to the season. It was a struggle to get her to go with him at Michaelmas."

He shrugged? The only response she was going to receive to such a comment was a shrug?

"He will be disappointed," Georgiana said softly.

"That cannot be helped."

Georgiana's heart sank at Darcy's words. Mr. Bingley had been so eager to return to Netherfield and a particular lady. In fact, he had mentioned taking his mother's fede ring with him when he returned. Not returning would do more than disappoint Mr. Bingley; it would likely break his heart and the heart of the lady he had left behind.

"Now, as delighted as I am to see you," her brother continued, "I am desirous of a long soak in a hot tub of water." He gave her a tight smile. "To wash away the chatter of Miss Bingley."

He had not remembered to ask her if she was well. That was also odd. For the last several months, he had asked her that question at least three times a day and always upon returning from a time away. She released his arm but only to allow her hand to slide down and grasp his.

"Fitzwilliam?" She waited until he looked up at her instead of at their joined hands before continuing. "Are you well?"

His eyes left hers and looked down the hall toward his room as he nodded. "I will be," he said as he lifted her hand and kissed her fingers. "I will be."

Georgiana pulled her lip between her teeth as she watched him walk down the hall to his room. His shoulders were not as square as they normally were, and he ran his hand through his hair which was something he only did when thoroughly overwhelmed by a situation. He was not well. Something was most certainly wrong.

Georgiana gasped as a reason for her brother's melancholy came to mind. Unwilling to entertain the troubling thought for hours before she spoke to her brother again, she hurried down the hall and knocked firmly on his door. Then she waited. There was some shuffling in the room, but none that sounded as if a person were approaching the door, so she knocked again. This time she rapt so loudly that she was positive at least one knuckle would bear a bruise from the action.

However, her sore knuckles had produced the

desired effect since her brother, minus his coat and cravat, opened his door.

"She has not trapped you, has she?" Georgiana demanded.

Her brother's brows drew together in question. "I beg your pardon?"

"Caroline Bingley. She has not finally succeeded in trapping you into marriage while her brother was gone, has she?" Georgiana's heart raced with trepidation. Caroline Bingley was not the sort of lady she wished to have as a sister, nor did she think her brother would ever be happy married to such a person. Caroline was not horrid, but she was not gentle or lively or particularly witty. She was just not the sort of lady Georgiana knew her brother needed for a wife.

Thankfully, shock suffused her brother's face as he blurted an emphatic no.

"You are not marrying her?" Georgiana asked again just to be certain of his answer.

"No, Georgie, I am not marrying anyone." The light in his eyes faded as he said it.

In spite of her concern for the sadness in his tone and expression, Georgiana smiled at him. "One day you will," she said hopefully.

"Perhaps one day," he replied without so much as a hint of conviction that it was true.

Oh, he was in a deplorable state of mind, and Georgiana was quite certain she knew why.

Acknowledgements

There are many who have had a part in the creation of this story. Some have read and commented on it. Some have proofread for grammatical errors and plot holes. Others have not even read the story and a few, I know, will never read it. However, their encouragement and belief in my ability, as well as their patience when I became cranky or when supper was late or the groceries ran low, was invaluable.

And so, I would like to say *thank you* to Zoe, Rose, Kristine, Ben, and Kyle, as well as Patrons at Patreon, who followed this story as it developed and waited, as patiently as one might do, from one Friday to the next to read a new chapter. I feel blessed through your help, support, and understanding.

I have not listed my dear husband in the above group because, to me, he deserves his own special thank you, for, without his somewhat pushy insistence that I start sharing my writing, none of my writing goals and dreams would have been met.

Other Leenie B Books

You can find all of Leenie's books at this link
bit.ly/LeenieBBooks
where you can explore the collections below

~*~

Other Pens, Mansfield Park

~*~

Touches of Austen Collection

~*~

Nature's Fury and Delights, Novelette Anthologies

~*~

Sweet Possibilities and Sweet Extras

~*~

Dash of Darcy and Companions Collection

~*~

Marrying Elizabeth Series

~*~

Willow Hall Romances

~*~

The Choices Series

~*~

Darcy Family Holidays

~*~

Teatime Tales Novelettes Collection

~*~

Darcy and... An Austen-Inspired Collection

About the Author

Leenie Brown has always been a girl with an active imagination, which, while growing up, was both an asset, providing many hours of fun as she played out stories, and a liability, when her older sister and aunt would tell her frightening tales. At one time, they had her convinced Dracula lived in the trunk at the end of the bed she slept in when visiting her grandparents!

Although it has been years since she cowered in her bed in her grandparents' basement, she still has an imagination which occasionally runs away with her, and she feeds it now as she did then — by reading!

Her heroes, when growing up, were authors, and the worlds they painted with words were (and still are) her favourite playgrounds! Now, as an adult, she spends much of her time in the Regency world, playing with the characters from her favourite Jane Austen novels and those of her own creation.

When she is not traipsing down a trail in an attempt to keep up with her imagination, Leenie resides in the beautiful province of Nova Scotia with her two sons and her very own Mr. Brown (a wonderful mix of all the best of Darcy, Bingley, and Edmund with a healthy dose of the teasing Mr. Tilney and just a dash of the scolding Mr. Knightley).

Connect with Leenie

E-mail:
LeenieBrownAuthor@gmail.com
Facebook:
www.facebook.com/LeenieBrownAuthor
Blog:
leeniebrown.com
Patreon:
https://www.patreon.com/LeenieBrown
Subscribe to Leenie's Mailing List:
Book News from Leenie Brown
(bit.ly/LeenieBBookNews)